Joyce Stranger is the author of many well-loved novels for both adults and children. She has always been associated with animals and has spent much of her life helping friends who farm or breed horses and dogs, as well as training her own dogs for Obedience shows. All the animal incidents in her books are based on her own experiences.

She and her husband live in Anglesey. They have two sons and a daughter, and many grandchildren.

'When she writes on animals, she shows a rare and living perception, presenting the creatures on their own terms as well as from the view of an observant and understanding human.'

—Naomi Lewis

'Joyce Stranger is rare among contemporary novelists in that her novels are always first and foremost enjoyable.'

—Richard Askwith,
Gamekeeper and Countryside

'Not only is Joyce Stranger a true animal lover but she is an excellent writer. Her books are always a pleasure to read.'

—Book Exchange

Also by Joyce Stranger

A DOG CALLED GELERT
LAKELAND VET
WALK A LONELY ROAD
CHIA THE WILDCAT
ZARA
BREED OF GIANTS
NEVER COUNT APPLES
CASEY
RUSTY
ONE FOR SORROW
REX
THE RUNNING FOXES
NEVER TELL A SECRET
FLASH
KYM
TWO'S COMPANY
THREE'S A PACK
A WALK IN THE DARK
THE JANUARY QUEEN
HOW TO OWN A SENSIBLE DOG

and published by Corgi Books

The Monastery Cat And Other Animals

Joyce Stranger

CORGI BOOKS

A DIVISION OF TRANSWORLD PUBLISHERS LTD

THE MONASTERY CAT AND OTHER ANIMALS

A CORGI BOOK 0 552 12044 8

First publication in Great Britain

PRINTING HISTORY
Corgi edition published 1982

This book is set in 10/11 Plantin

Corgi Books are published by Transworld Publishers Ltd.,
Century House, 61–63 Uxbridge Road, Ealing, London W5 5SA

Made and printed in Great Britain by
Hunt Barnard Printing Ltd, Aylesbury, Bucks.

The Monastery Cat And Other Animals

CONTENTS

THE MONASTERY CAT

The monastery was perched on a cliff, high in the mountains.

In summer the holy Fathers looked down from an eagle perch on sweeping columns of dark pine trees which stretched all the way to the distant village huddled in a valley, where steep roofs were aligned to shed the winter snow.

In winter the world was masked with white. The sun glittered on sheets of snow. There was no relief from the stark lack of colour.

It was quiet in the monastery.

The days passed without incident. The holy Fathers rose early to pray, before starting the day's work. Father Anselm was in charge of the goats who provided milk and butter and cheese. Often he wished that there were other animals. He was a farmer's son and he hungered for the care of a herd of cows; for sheep; for dogs to lighten the day, and most of all a cat.

But he dared not ask for a cat.

Father Jerome was in charge of the gardens where he grew all the vegetables that were needed. He too liked animals, and missed them, so that often he helped milk the goats, and enjoyed working in the big sheds where the three nannies lived. Each year the farmer in the village brought his Billy up the mountain, and each year there were three kids to liven the days. Some years there were twins.

The Fathers never left the monastery. They watched the eagle soar high above them; they watched the ant people in the village below. They had little chance to sin. Their sins were sins of anger, and of envy; of greed, when food became all-important as there was so little to mark the passing days; of spite against one another, living too close together, being human, and not saints, as they would have wished.

Their pleasure came from song. Sometimes, on a very clear day, the villagers could hear the Fathers singing, and the sonorous notes of the organ, drifting down the mountains, sounded like a choir of angels, high above them. They paused to listen and to smile at one another.

The villagers also heard the monastery bell. It marked the hours and it was rung for meals, and the villagers timed their clocks by it. Its silver chime sounded over the village like a benison, and the notes floated on the air.

Life in the monastery had gone on unchanging for so long that sometimes Father Anselm wondered if he were becoming mummified. Longings for the world outside assailed him and he had to confess that he was not entirely tuned to the holy life that he should be leading. He had been very young when he joined the Order.

And now he was growing old and wondered if he had truly found his vocation.

The longing for animals was so strong that he spent more time than was necessary among the goats. Each one was a character, and he had named them all. He grieved when they died and he rejoiced when the kids were born, thanking God for the repeated miracle of life.

One winter morning he left the goats and walked slowly across the snow-covered yard. He felt rebellious, and longed to open the gate and stride down the mountain and snatch some of the life that he had missed. Shock at his thoughts stopped him in mid-stride and he looked up at the blue sky and prayed that the Lord would forgive him for his frailty.

He would go into the chapel and pray for his restlessness to leave him.

The tiny chapel was beside the big gate. That was rarely opened. It blocked out the world, a massive oak gate, thick-planked and iron-studded. Sometimes it reminded him of a prison door.

Outside the gate, a baby cried.

Shocked, Father Anselm stood and stared. Surely no

one had brought a child to the holy Fathers. What on earth would they do? The cry came again, a long wailing sobbing call that brought some of the other Fathers running. Father Anselm opened the gate.

There in the snow was not a baby, but a tiny Siamese kitten. Its small back was bloodstained; its blue eyes stared up at them and it wailed pitifully.

'What man has done this?' Father Jerome asked angrily.

Father Anselm looked at the unmarked snow. He looked upwards, at the eagle soaring above.

'No man,' he said.

'Are you suggesting this is a miracle?' Father Jacques asked in a shocked voice. He was writing a book about miracles, and saw the hand of God in many ways; but not in the advent of a battered kitten from outer space.

'The eagle snatched it and dropped it,' Father Anselm said. 'Perhaps God had a hand in it too. He moves in mysterious ways.'

He lifted the kitten and Father Jerome closed the great gate.

The talons had cut deep, but the kitten was strong. He purred and rubbed his small head against Father Anselm's cheek, and the monk knew at once that he could not part with this morsel of life. He was afraid the Abbot would forbid them to keep the kitten, but the Abbot came to look, and touched the small creature and smiled.

'He came to us for succour and that he will have,' he said.

Father Anselm dressed the injuries with the ointment that he had bought from the apothecary for one of the goats; he fed him with bread and milk, and he found a wooden box in a corner of the goat shed and scrubbed it clean.

Father Jerome remembered that there were old blankets in the big armoire on the stairs of the passage that led to the monks' spartan cells. He cut one of the worst worn into pieces, and he found a stone bottle and filled it with warm water. The little cat would be suffering from shock.

The kitten did not intend to sleep in his box.

He had been snatched from his mother, as he played

in the sun; he had been carried miles into the air, the great talons digging cruelly into his fur. He had summoned all his strength and twisted upwards and slashed with needle-like claws at the bird's feathered legs and had drawn blood. The eagle, startled by the unexpected attack, had dropped his prey.

Father Anselm looked at the kitten. He was about three months old; his fur was cream; his paws and tail and mask were a delicate grey-blue; his eyes were as vivid as the gentians that grew in the summer pastures.

They named him Ciel because he had dropped from the sky.

Ciel soon became part of the monastery's routine. His small agile body was to be seen trotting busily along the passages; exploring the cells, visiting each monk in turn, giving some his favours by day, and others by night. The box and the blanket remained by the big fire in the kitchen, but the Fathers kept Ciel's night-time visits a dark secret. He slept now on one bed, now on another, and those who were honoured by his visits spent idle moments teasing him with a straw, on which he pounced, or pulling their rope girdles along the ground, watching him dart like quicksilver.

There was often laughter among the monks as Ciel danced with his shadow, or pounced on imaginary mice. He loved to leap on to the big dresser, or to the top of the armoire, and jump on to the unwary as they passed beneath so that when there was a sudden startled shout the brothers laughed and looked at one another and said,

'Oh that Ciel. He's done it again.'

Ciel killed the rats that lived even here on the mountain, attracted by the stored sacks of food. He killed the mice, and the monastery had never been so free from vermin.

'He earns his place,' Father Anselm often said. The monks repeated themselves on many occasions as there was so little to discuss.

Ciel even invaded the chapel but here he seemed to know he must not make a noise or play. He curled himself neatly on a pew and listened to the singing. He loved song, and sometimes, very wickedly, Father Anselm sang one of his boyhood ballads, songs of knights and ladies, and of rivers flowing swiftly through green fields; of lakes and of pastures, and he sang the song his grandfather had sung when milking the cows. He often sang it to the goats to bring their milk more swiftly.

Kitty coo, kitty coo, kitty coo milking,
Let down your milk, let down your milk,
Kitty coo, milking.

Ciel would lie on his knee and look up at him wide-eyed, intent, with a stare that seemed to lay bare his soul. Then the monk would laugh and tickle the cat and the cat would turn on his back and attack the big brown fist in mock battle, pretending to scratch and stab, but always keeping the long lethal claws sheathed.

Sometimes he rode on Father Anselm's shoulder. He did this for no one else and some of the monks were just a little jealous, enticing the cat with titbits from their plates, and even lifting him to sit beside their ears, but Ciel would have none of that.

He went his own way, and no one could change him.

He had been with the monks three years. He had learned that every meal time was heralded by the sound of the bell, and he knew that then the holy Fathers left their chores and took their wooden dishes and went to the cook for their portions. They fed sparsely, on porridge and rye bread for breakfast; on a stew of vegetables with very little meat at lunch, with rye bread and cheese for dessert; and at supper they dined on eggs and bread and drank the goats' milk.

Ciel shared their food, and when the long procession filed through the corridors towards the refectory, the little cat led it, marching sedately, tail erect, occasionally looking back to see that everyone was following him. Even the Abbot had to laugh at their leader, and his small self-assurance, and no one knew that sometimes when the wind blew eerily round the corners, alarming the little cat, Ciel found his way to the Abbot's warm room, where the old man slept for so little a while. He would spend half the night in prayer, with a small furry body tucked against his knees, under his robes, hiding from the wind, delighted to find a human awake and able to protect him from the invisible demons that strode outside the monastery walls, yelling their anger.

One morning the bell rang, and no cat appeared. The holy Fathers stared at one another. Who had seen him last? Where had he spent the night? Only then did they find that Ciel distributed his favours impartially and at one time or another had slept on every bed in the monastery. But that night no one had seen him. No one had seen him since supper the day before.

They searched the monastery. It was so easy for a little cat bent on mischief to run before them and hide. They searched the cupboards and the goat shed; they searched their drawers and their small possessions; they stared at the great gate, wondering if Ciel could have climbed it and gone outside.

But it was winter and there were no tracks in the snow.

Father Anselm looked up.

The eagle was soaring overhead.

He shook his fist at the devil bird. There was their answer. The kitten they had saved three years ago had fallen victim in the end.

There were no smiles on the bearded faces, and the voices that sang that day were sad. Father Anselm moved the little box; Father Jerome hid the small dish that always held Ciel's food. Fathers in every cell in the monastery hid the telltale pieces of string with which they played with the cat.

The solemn procession that led down the corridor to the refectory moved slowly, as if at a funeral, and the Abbot chided himself for missing so small a part of his routine. It was only a cat....

But they thought they saw Ciel dancing with his shadow and they heard his wails.

Three days passed.

Father Anselm still longed for the cat. He missed the muscular little body that raced through the shadows, or played in the goat shed, or leaped from the cupboards. He still thought he could hear wails and chided himself for an over-active imagination.

Breakfast was over on the third day and all the monks were about their daily business. The bell would not sound again until lunch-time.

The villagers too were about their daily business, the men at their work, the women chatting as they shopped for the family's food.

It would be two hours before the chime sounded on the mountain.

Suddenly they heard the bell.

The schoolchildren ran outside and stared up at the monastery. The shopkeepers and the women raced into the village street, for this was no silver chime, but an angry clang clang that went on and on endlessly.

Was the monastery on fire?

Had a monk died, and another monk, overcome by grief, gone mad as he clanged the angry bell?

There was no smoke.

There was no sign of turmoil.

But there was turmoil.

Father Anselm left the goat in mid-milking and she kicked the bucket over and flooded her pen. Father Jerome dropped the bucket of water he was carrying and injured his toe. The Abbot, at prayer, stood suddenly and knocked over his precious cup, the only possession that he had brought from the world outside. It was a very ordinary cup, but he was sad when it broke as it was a link with a childhood he had almost forgotten.

The cook forgot the stew and left the flame too high.

The monks ran.

They picked up their skirts and raced to the bell room, and counted heads as they ran. All were there. So who was ringing the bell? Had the devil come in person to punish them for wickedness? Or was there a demon or hobgoblin there in the empty room?

They stopped at the door, afraid to go in. The Abbot pushed them aside. He was an old man, and his long beard was white. He faltered when he walked, but he was their spiritual leader and he alone would challenge the demons of the dark.

He flung the door open.

There was a roar of laughter such as had never been heard in the monastery before.

For there, clinging to the bell rope, swinging to and fro, was Ciel, covered in dust and fluff, his fur bristling, his eyes angry. He was starving and he had been to the refectory and found they had forgotten his plate of food. He could not find any of the holy Fathers, and he knew that food always came when the bell was rung, so he had rung the bell.

He dropped from the rope and led the way to the refectory and a hilarious procession followed him, the cook racing to the kitchen to bring milk and meat, the holy Fathers rejoicing that their pet was found.

Father Guiseppe, who came from Italy, was the cook. He brought meat and he brought milk and he brought goat cheese, knowing that Ciel loved it, and they stood around, forgetting their duties, watching the cat.

He finished his food.

He was cold. Very cold.

He stalked to the kitchen and wailed because his box had vanished. Father Anselm brought it from the cupboard and filled the stone bottle and Ciel tucked himself down. Father Jerome brought a damp cloth and dusted the dirty fur.

Where could he have been?

Down in the village the people shrugged. The holy Fathers had gone mad, but that was not surprising, seeing the life they led, isolated there on the mountain. It was more than men could endure. It was some weeks before the villagers settled, as they were expecting to hear again the crazy clanging of the angry bells, instead of the soft chimes that marked the passing hours.

They forgot.

The monks did not forget. Father Jerome, going into the cellar for stores, which were kept there in the cool, found the dusty floor in the rarely used far cellar, marked with a cat's frantic paws as he had paced trying desperately to find a way of escape. He must have run down in the dark while they were carrying up the sacks, and gone unnoticed into the further room and been shut in.

That accounted for the mysterious wails that everyone had heard, but that no one admitted to hearing.

Ciel took great care never to venture into the cellars again.

He was treasured as no cat ever was treasured, becoming old and wise, making life in the remote mountains happier than it could ever have been without his presence.

Father Martin, who loved to draw, painted a picture of a small cat clinging to a thick rope; the picture was hung in one of the corridors, where everyone passed it, and smiled a reminiscent smile of pleasure at the memory.

No one thought to enlighten the villagers and to this day they still wonder and talk about the day when the holy Fathers went mad and the chimes of the bell angered the air, sounding at the wrong time, uttering a devils' carillon that had no tune and no meaning.

THE DOG THIEF

Sabre was bored.

He hated kennels more than he hated anything else in life, but he knew it was useless to complain, as the other dogs were complaining, their barks making the daytime horrible. At night, most of them slept, except for a small whippet that fretted and whimpered. Sometimes she crept close to the wire that separated her from the big police dog, and Sabre licked her nose, and she gained comfort.

He looked about him, hoping against hope that his handler might come for him and release him from this misery of inaction. He was a working dog, and work was his life. Work was his joy, his meaning for existence, and he always gave his best, with a wealth of affection that overflowed from his abounding generosity.

He had been in kennels often before. But he never grew

resigned. He wanted to be out on the beat, watching, listening, eager, with his handler beside him, and the busy sounds of life around him.

It was Sunday morning, and on Sundays the dogs were fed, but not exercised. Today there would be no romp with Sally in the yard. Today there would be nothing, without end. Sabre lay down, his nose on his paws, his brown eyes watching for the man who would not come. Even policemen had holidays.

The Alsatian was not fretting. He knew, from experience, that in time he would be released for activity. He had always been released before, and learned to trust the man with whom he lived and worked. He could only wait.

Sally was on duty alone. Sally was eighteen, slim, with shining hair that flowed over her shoulders. Her small face was insignificant except for long brown eyes under straight black brows, eyes that were as expressive as a dog's and that spoke to the dogs in a way that they understood.

She was shy, and afraid of the rough boys who lived near her. She was especially afraid of Len, with his dark hair that grew to his shoulders. Shoulders made even more broad by a leather jacket covered in bright tabs. His dark eyes mocked her, and so did his swaggering assurance that no girl could ever resist his charms.

Sally had run from him on several occasions, panicked by his manner, by his strong brown hands that crushed her arms as he tried to snatch a kiss, by his insistence that one day she would give in to him, and, then, then, he'd show her.

She hated him and was afraid of him and of the gang he went around with, all of them speeding on fast motor bikes with girls who incited them to ever more daring exploits. Somehow, none of these girls appealed to Len. They were all too easy. Easy come, easy go. It was Sally that attracted him, Sally and her slender figure and wide frightened eyes, and her way of running from him. He had had a kitten once with eyes like that. He had loved it for a week, and then had drowned it, holding it under the water, smiling at its terrified struggles. He did not want to drown Sally, but he knew what he wanted to do with her and he knew that she would struggle. The very thought quickened his breath.

He followed her whenever he saw her. She could no longer walk on the downs, where the wind was clean and the birds sang and there was quiet. She could no longer walk on the beach, and sit alone on a rock watching the sea cover the sand and daydream, about the horse she would one day own, and the poems that would one day be published and that came into her mind as she sat, conscious of the scent of seaweed and the wind's moan and the pounding waves. The words stemmed from excitement at life and wild places, and they died, choked by terror, when Len came towards her, having watched her leave home. She was always running now.

She craved quiet. She lived in a tiny house with three noisy sisters, and there was never any peace. She stood beside the kennel, looking at Sabre. She needed him. He would protect her. With him she would be safe, and could walk alone again, in her favourite places. Not even Len could stand up against the dog.

No one was about. She had fed all the animals and cleaned the floors, and was trusted to lock up. The family were in church, and Mr. Stanton, who owned the kennels, had gone with them, knowing Sally would not fail in any of her duties. If she took Sabre out on the downs no one would ever know. She could bring him back safely before their return. Her desire to walk was so great that she could not deny it.

She fetched Sabre's lead. He saw her come back, recognised his own property and was at once on his feet, tail wagging, bounding with excitement. He sat, while she fastened the clip. She would not let go of him or let him wander, just in case she lost him, and he failed to return to the kennels but went off to his own home to look for his handler.

No one saw them leave by the high gate in the brick wall. There was freedom in the morning for both of them. A lark sang overhead. No one was about. She ran, her feet flying over the mossy grass, and the dog beside her, elated with living.

* * *

Sunday, for Len, was also an island of boredom. He was not meeting any of the gang till the afternoon. He waited outside the kennels, knowing Sally must come out soon and determined to waylay her. Boredom had sparked off determination and the boarding kennels were isolated. He walked round the high wall and saw the girl and dog in the distance, up on the downs. At the same time he saw Sam, who was as bored as Len. They were both members of the same gang. He pointed to Sally, and Sam grinned and the two of them began to run.

They ran swiftly and silently, trying to head her off, but they had reckoned without the dog. Sabre heard them and smelt them, and Sally was alerted by his threatening growl. She turned her head, and fear grabbed her throat and panic took her. Sabre could not deal with two of them at once.

She ran over the soft ground, towards the cliffs above the sea, and behind her she heard the noise of thudding feet, nightmare realised, so that her breath rasped her throat and she longed to scream.

She topped the rise. There were people in the distance, but none of them was close enough to see her predicament. She turned, the sea behind her lulling softly, the gulls above her wheeling and screaming, and terror faced her as Len came towards her, grinning his wild grin, his hair flying behind him in the wind.

He reached out his hand and Sabre sprang. Sam, panicking, threw a knife at the dog. It missed, and hit the ground. The dog backed away, barking furiously, barking to alert the handler who was not there, barking to inspire fear, barking to gain time. Sally crouched, terrified. Len jumped to his feet and Sam circled, trying to reach his knife, but the dog was always in the way.

The people in the distance heard the dog, saw the crouching girl and the two lads, and four men ran, pounding over the turf. Sam and Len saw them coming and ran too, and Sabre gave chase, determined to keep them from escaping. He jumped again at Len, sensing that he was the greater danger. Sam reached for his knife, furious, and flung it again, so that it grazed Sally's arm. She was the cause of their trouble.

The sting of the cut and the sight of blood and the noise of pursuit and the barking dog sent Sally beyond the edge of reason. She couldn't bear the thought of the trouble that she had caused; she knew that there was more trouble to come as now Mr. Stanton would know she had taken Sabre. To take any dog out of the kennels was an unforgivable sin, and to take Sabre, of all of them, made the sin ten times worse. There was no dog like Sabre and he was valued, not only for his financial worth, but for his skill and cleverness. He was without possibility of replacement, gentle, affectionate, and with a sense of humour that endeared him to everyone, and that was all his own.

Sally knew that she would lose her job, and she loved her job more than she loved anything in the world. Her parents disliked animals, and had little sympathy when she announced that she would not be a hairdresser like Joan, or a secretary like Susan, or work in a dress shop like Kath. Her family could not understand her, and laughed at her, but in the end she was allowed to have her own way.

It was not easy, or romantic, working among the dogs. The cleaning up was horrible, and at times the chore of dish-washing and floor-scrubbing was wearisome in the extreme, but the dogs were her reward, eager, delighted when she groomed and played with them, enjoying every moment of the romps she had in the big wired compound where they could race and run safely, without fear of escape. Her high spirits when she was with them made her invaluable, and few owners had cause to complain that their pets came home miserable or under-exercised. Those that fretted Sally cuddled and loved, and coaxed to eat, until they accepted her as a new and pleasant part of their lives, and began to relax in their unfamiliar surroundings.

She thought of the dogs under her care now; of Snip, the whippet, that she and Sabre were curing of fretting; of little curly-coated Jasper, a bright-eyed and delightful chocolate-coloured poodle with a wicked sense of mischief;

and Sam, the golden retriever, waiting aloof for his mistress to return, but rewarding Sally with a solemn wag of his tail, knowing that she was there for his benefit, so that he barked at her when she passed, asking for a caress. And little Moss, the Border collie, contented enough in his own pen with the dogs that lived at home with him, Sandy the labrador, and the corgi, Rufus.

There were also the cats. Chloe and Kym, both Siamese, and Miche, a tiny black cat with wide amber eyes, and Tiger, a delightful marmalade tabby. Sally played with them, dragging a string for them to catch, or rolling a ball or a piece of screwed-up paper, ensuring each was exercised. The Stantons would never let her come back now. And no other job was worth having.

She could not see for the tears that misted her eyes. Behind her she heard voices, but dared not go back. She wished she were not so timid, that she could stand up for herself, like Joan, or boss people about, like Susan. It was no use. She had never been able to face up to things. She had always taken the line of least resistance. She had always run away from danger and from unpleasantness. Perhaps if she had not, she would know how to stand up to Len, but she was too frightened of him. She had seen him twisting his companions' arms and once watched him, in a milk bar, burn a boy of about ten with the end of his cigarette and laugh, while his companions laughed with him. The child was much too terrified of retaliation to tell anyone how he came by the burn, and Len, as always, went free. And Sally was too afraid of Len to tell anyone either.

She was too preoccupied to notice where she was going. The sounds had stopped behind her, and she slowed, panting, but she slowed too late. Her foot slipped, and the cliff edge was near and she rolled towards it. She cried out, but there was no one to hear, and she clutched desperately at the grass as she fell.

The men had reached Len and Sam. Sabre, infuriated, was racing from one to the other, snapping and growling, never coming in close, never biting. He had no need. His ferocious appearance was enough to panic both lads. One man picked the knife up, noting the bloodstain on the blade. It was a wicked thing, honed to razor shaprness. It was simple enough to grab Len and Sam, while Sabre marched beside them, snarling every time they moved incautiously. They soon learned to keep quiet. One of the men telephoned the police, and Sabre waited with them until the familiar car came into sight, and the familiar figures jumped out. Then, before anyone could stop him, the dog bolted towards the downs.

He had to find Sally. He was in charge of her, and he had lost her. Until she was safe, he could not rest. He ran over the ground, retracing his steps, until he came to the scene of the fight. He cast around, looking for Sally's scent.

It was easy to find. Bruised earth and broken grass, crushed thyme and crushed clover led him unerringly until he came to the edge of the cliff where she had fallen. He looked down. The edge had crumbled away, and far below was the sea, beating relentlessly against the chalk. Eight feet below the broken edge was a grassy ledge, and here Sally lay, her right ankle sprained and useless. She had crawled back across the grass until she lay against the sheer cliff, not daring to look down. Sabre barked.

Sally lifted a tear-stained face. She could not climb up and he could not climb down. The dog cast around, trying to find a way, but it was hopeless. He needed help, and to Sabre, help could only be gained from one place. There was only one set of men who would understand him.

The station sergeant was astounded when the dog raced into the room and barked at him. The man knew Sabre, and knew too that he was in kennels, or had been. But he also knew the Alsatian well enough to be aware that the animal was trying to convey information.

The sergeant came to the other side of the desk, and Sabre, desperate, grabbed the man's wrist and tried to lead him to the door.

'All right, old boy. We'll see what's up,' the man said.

He picked up the phone.

'I've got Sabre here. He's upset about something. Come and take my place and I'll follow him and see what's amiss.'

Sabre could not bear to wait. He ran to the door and looked back. He barked, and ran back and nosed the man's leg. At last the man was free to follow the dog. A police car was waiting to pick him up, and the two men left Sabre free to run along the pavement and drove slowly beside him, out of the town, past the kennels and on to the downs.

They left the car and followed on foot. Sabre knew the way. He bounded on, looking back again and again to make sure the men were there, desperately anxious to lead them to Sally.

Sally, lying against the cliff, listening to the scream of the gulls and beat of the sea, felt sick with pain and fright. When Sabre appeared again above her head, and barked at her, all hope left her. She had hoped, when he vanished, that he had gone for help. Now she knew he could not have done so.

'All right, love. We'll soon have you out of there.'

The sergeant's voice made Sally jump. But his tone was reassuring and she stared up at him, her eyes wide with disbelief.

'My mate's radioing for ropes. Lie still, and you'll be O.K. Does that leg hurt?'

Sally nodded, and then she screamed. Sabre had jumped, over the edge of the cliff. She saw his falling body come towards her. He landed on the ledge and licked her face, his tail waving extravagantly. She put her arms around him, holding on to him, shaking with relief. If he had been killed....

Half an hour later, she was safe, lying on the cliff top, while Sabre sat waiting for the praise he knew was due. By now Mr. Stanton had discovered his most precious charge was missing, and, going to the police station to report his loss, had met the rescue car. He knelt beside Sally, trying to stop the sobs that shook her.

'It's O.K. love. It's O.K. love,' a young constable was repeating. He too had often seen Sally and watched her, liking her quietness and the shyness which made her different from the cheeky girls he often met. He lifted her now, to carry her to the waiting police car. It was good to have done a satisfactory job, to have a happy ending. And they had that little rat Len, and Sam with him. Both of them would get what they deserved. He tightened his hold on Sally. If Len had got at her. . . . The constable looked down at the hair that lay on his arm, a small smile on his mouth. He liked shy girls, and he hadn't got a girl of his own. The other blokes laughed at him. Well, maybe he'd have one now, and maybe he could interview her and find out why she had taken Sabre, though he could guess, at that.

That night, as Sally lay on the couch at home, watching television, he called on her, bringing her a book to read while she was laid up. No one else was in, and Sally, without her family's criticising gaze, relaxed, and lost some of her shyness.

'What about your job?' he asked her.

'Mr Stanton says I can stay, just as long as I don't take Sabre out again,' Sally said. 'He did understand when I told him. He was very nice about it.'

She sighed.

'It's miserable, never being able to walk anywhere without being scared of lads being after you,' she said.

'You like the downs?' the constable asked her.

She nodded.

'It's quiet up there, and you can think,' she said. 'I like quiet places. Only they're always so lonely.'

'I like quiet places too,' the constable said. 'As soon as that ankle's better, suppose you show me some of them? And I'll tell you something else. I've been accepted as a dog handler too, and I'm going to get a dog. His name's Wolf, and he's one of Sabre's pups. He won't be like Sabre. There isn't another dog like Sabre, but he'll be quite a dog, and we can take him with us when we go walking. He'll need the exercise. You'll like that.'

Sally looked at him thoughtfully. She would like that, and some of the uneasiness and distrust lifted from her.

'I'll be back,' the constable said.

Sally thought of a future in which she had a dog of her own and perhaps a man of her own, and smiled to herself, while back in kennels Sabre stared at the sky. He had had quite a day, but he was bored again and he wished someone would come for him so that he could run free and work and be with his own people. He sighed.

The whippet whimpered, lonely for her home and the warm bed in which she slept and the familiar voices that soothed her. She stretched herself against the wire, and Sabre lay close so that some of his warmth reached her. She thrust her nose towards him and he licked her face through the mesh, and the moon shone down on both of them as they slept, unaware that tomorrow would end their uncomplaining vigil, and that tomorrow they would be home again. Sally would miss them, but other dogs would claim her care.

THE WILD WHITE HORSES

It was Christmas Eve.

The world was alight with excitement. Children fretted at the slowly passing hours. They made plans and bought presents, and huddled in corners, glowing, as they whispered secrets. Parents glanced at each other with meaning in their eyes. Strange shaped parcels, gaily wrapped, were hidden in odd corners and put on high shelves, and tucked into drawers, insecurely masked by piled shirts or underwear.

The excitement spilled into the seething last-minute streets, where, at night, bright lights glittered. From every lamp post angels danced. Unicorns, splendid in silver and gold, shone above the slowly moving motor cars. Children gazed skywards at giant crowns, jewelled with glory, and Santa Claus sat on his sleigh, his reindeer lifting their antlers high above Market Street.

Shop windows were hung with tinsel, and snow covered the floor inside, while mannequins, in their Christmas splendour, sledged, wrapped in furs, or held pretty baubles towards the idling crowds. Frost flecked the glass. Christmas trees shimmered with shining balls, and small children, faces flushed with cold, pressed their noses against the icy panes and, with eyes brighter than the brilliant balls, lost themselves in a maze of delight.

Market Street was a solid mass of people, homeward bound, hurrying to the bus station and the railway station, anxious to get home, away from the cold, to start preparing for the next day, the greatest day of all, for feast and for fun and for the early present giving. Few of them noticed the three gypsy girls with their long black tangled hair and brown faces and bright patched shawls of orange and green and blue, clutching their baskets. The girls had saved their money so that they could come to Manchester to shop and to see the big city for the first time, and moreover, see it in all its Christmas splendour. They were in no hurry and going nowhere and had all the time in the world. They looked up at lights that dazzled along the street, and looked down at mock snow and fake frost on shop window floors, and looked in at every scene set to attract and excite them, unaware that this was to lure the people inside and help them spend their money. They had no money left to spend, nor did it occur to them to be envious.

They walked through Piccadilly Gardens, where luminous plaster owls lurked in the trees and goblins peeped from the bushes, enchanting the children, and coloured lights hung, unusual exotic winter fruits, from slender branches. They paused to look at a snow house and a snowman, seeming more real then snow itself. They crossed the road, moving with the throng, unnerved by traffic that snarled and fought its way down the main roads and turned off at every corner, often baulked by the mass of pedestrians attempting to cross from side to side, eyes on the lights above them and not on the streets in front of them. The gypsy girls were thin and ragged and undernourished but laughter was never far from their mouths, and their merry voices and quick movement caught many eyes as they moved through the busy throng. Their world today was an infinite satisfaction, as brave and colourful as any gypsy's wildest dream. The girls asked for nothing and expected nothing. It was enough to look, to caress with every glance, to fold the glory and wonder away in the mind where it could remain. At a later date they would bring it from their treasure house and revel afresh in the colour and excitement and brilliance of a world to which they could never belong and whose splendour they could only admire from outside.

It began to snow. Large flakes drifted slowly through the air, and the city dirt was masked in shining white. Flakes settled on hair and cheek and shoulder, drifted down onto the side street barrows of gold and green fruit, and on those which were massed with yellow and red tawny flowers. The stragglers hurried, anxious for warm fire and tea and television set. Children wailed, hungry and fretful. The girls watched them and smiled. There were small ones at home, inside the brightly painted caravans. They too were preparing for Christmas. They did not want to hasten back. They would wait and see the night-time crowds and sleep, huddled together for warmth, in some arched doorway, or perhaps, if they were lucky, find a deserted hayloft outside the city. They had shopped for Christmas. Romaine had bought her mother a shining brooch, a beautiful thing of glass and beads, the cluster as bright as any real gem in any jeweller's window. She held it in her hand, wrapped in tissue paper, more precious than diamonds, Sarina had found a tinsel scarf that would brighten her married sister's hair. Both her parents were dead, and her sister looked after her. She had also a bag of tiny sweets for her baby niece. Anita had found a fluffy horse, all of four inches high, made of white brushed-up felt, with a curled black wool mane and bright black eyes and nose. A minute scarlet saddle added an air of gaiety. Her little sister would love the toy.

The girls turned into a side street. The high walls closed together and the lights were gone. They had entered a black canyon, lit by the soft glow from one lamp, which illuminated the falling flakes. A black and white timbered building cast its shadow on the cobbles and loured against the dark as it had when Shakespeare was a boy. The windows glowed gold, and voices from the public house spilled into the darkness. The girls moved to catch the warmth from the doorway and savour the smell of frying chips that came from the kitchen.

It was then that they saw the pony. He was tethered to a post. A creamy pony with gold mane and tail, trembling with cold and weariness and hunger. His large wise eyes shone with tears caused by the icy wind that cut into him. The girls stopped.

Anita put her arms about his neck and leaned against him. She was warm and she smelled of comfort and love and his tired tense body relaxed. He was not used to kindness. Her small hand fondled his mane.

'He is just like my pony. See?' she said, and held the toy up to the light. The pony huffed at her.

He was a gentle creature, and life was wearying for him. He found the world a frightening place.

His master drove a cart. Each morning the cream pony was caught, groomed roughly and carelessly, and put between the shafts, where he stood, dejected, until a whip was laid spitefully across his shoulders.

His hooves were painful, needing paring, and he clip-clopped along in shoes lacking a nail, so that often he was lame, but not lame enough for his master to know or care.

Sometimes a bright balloon was tied to his harness, to attract the children who swarmed on his route. He hated it. He hated the flabby feel and the bat, bat, bat against his neck when he trotted, and even worse, the terrifying bang when some boy, grinning with mischief, punctured it with a pin, or a man pushed a glowing cigarette butt against it.

He hated the days spent dragging a cart that became heavier and heavier as the hours went by: and the evenings standing in the rain and mud in the seven-acre field where the grass grew thin and spare and thistly and the food his master gave him was sparse and stale.

He longed for lush green grass, for the feel of summer meadow, rich with buttercups, beneath his tired hooves, and the dip and trickle of running water, remembered dimly from a time long ago when freedom had been his. Freedom to gallop under a summer sun, to roll in long, clean grass, and stand swishing his tail against the flies, fetlock deep in cool clear water where tiny fish arrowed in darting flight brushed against his legs, tickling them.

The pony had often stood with his head over the gate, longing for a human to stop and give him a kind word, or a titbit, and he had grown more and more sorrowful. His head had drooped, his tail had hung behind him, useless for flicking flies as it had been docked by his master who objected to a swishing tail in front of him all day.

Slowly the years had passed. The pony had wilted, finding no pleasure in living. How should he? His days were spent trotting on hard roads, the whip ever ready to flick at his shoulders. At night he had grown too tired to run in the seedy field. Sometimes he had watched the moon slide over the sky, and leaves, moon-flecked, shiver in the wind.

When the wind had blown he had turned his tail to it and stood patient, feeling the strange unseen creature ruffle his hair and tease his mane, tangling it even more. He had longed for someone to brush the grit from his coat and smooth the jagged tangles in mane and tail, and he had sighed more deeply as the years went by.

He had also longed for company. Another pony to lean against, and lick in friendship; to run against, and to call joyously when he had come back from the streets at night.

He had nothing.

Now he looked at the girls, feeling the friendship that radiated from them, warming him. He leaned his head against Romaine, who was standing in front of him, crooning to him as no one had crooned in his life before, and he pushed her gently, wishing he could communicate both his gratitude and his need.

Snow was drifting over them. The pony shook his head, hating it. He yearned for food, for warmth, for love and for kindness, for an owner who would groom him and soothe him and comfort him, for a warm stable and for hay that smelled of summer, and not of damp and mould.

Romaine put both her arms round him and he turned his head and nuzzled her with velvet lips. His brown eyes gazed at her, wishing that he could be hers, that her gentle hands might always stroke his coat and play with his mane, that he might be free for ever of the rumbling jolting cart that dragged behind him uphill and chased after him downhill and always hurt his back. He longed to be free of the confining chafing harness that made him sore, and of the hateful batting balloon.

'We ought to do something about him,' Romaine said.

Sarina and Anita looked at her. The alleyway was dark, light from the street lamp spilling onto the pony's head. The cart, piled high with old clothes, with tyres, with bits and pieces once treasured and now discarded, was in deep shadow. They gave the pony a last kiss each, then one by one they crept under the old clothes, making no sound, showing neither face nor arm nor hand.

The man came out of the public house, stumbling and swearing. He fumbled at the reins and when the pony did not acknowledge him, slapped its neck. The pony breathed sadly and softly and dropped his head lower. He did not want to start again, did not want to pull the heavy cart, did not want to clop over the cobbles, with the wind knifing at him. The snow had turned to rain, which had just begun to fall, wetting him.

The man clambered onto the cart, tugged at the reins, and slashed with his whip. The pony moved, heaving with his shoulders, feeling the weight of the cart. The wheels gripped and began to turn.

They walked out of the alley and into the main traffic. Cars sped past him, and a policeman looked at him sourly. He was holding up all the traffic behind him. Hooters sounded, and men glared at him when they found room to overtake him. Children looked back, seeing not an old and shabby pony, but a dream horse, piebald and beautiful, his head looking towards them, mild eyed, the gay balloon a banner at his neck, the man a figure of mystery, as he drove through the night.

The rain, which had succeeded the snow, turned once more to sleet, and finally to snow again. Huge wet flakes drifted down and the trees were masked and shone in the lamplight. The world turned from everyday to fairytale magic and houses lay secret under whitened roofs, and hedges and roads alike were smooth and beautiful. The thud of the dragging hooves was muffled, and the pony slipped, and stopped. The flicking spiteful whip drove him on again.

The girls, warm under the old clothes, but almost stifled by the dust and stuffy smell of them, peeped out through the cracks, and watched the world they knew change. In the fields where the caravans stood, there would be even more beauty for all the daytime mud would be hidden, while the silent snow turned the trees to Christmas glory.

They clopped on. The traffic was less. Most people were home by now, and the road beyond Fallowfield station stretched broad and quiet. The shops were closed, some of them lit for Christmas, so that trees and tinsel and shining baubles glittered invitingly.

It seemed a long journey to the girls and even longer to the pony. He thought of food, hung in bags for him to tug, of grass, long and green and luscious, of water, and of sunshine and warmth. He shivered. Other creatures would spend the night indoors, but his only shelter was a shed without a door to it and with only half a roof and with the floor sodden. He had little protection from the weather. If he was lucky there might be some mouldy hay bought cheap because it was useless to anyone else. He would have to dig through the snow and nose out the grass that remained in the muddy field. He was cold and he was hungry and he was tired. His hooves dragged but the whip stung his neck again so he speeded his pace. Once he got the man home the cart would be removed and the chafing harness hung on the wall and there would be a little moment of peace before the galls that chafed him began to hurt again, and hunger remind him of his misery.

When they reached Didsbury they turned by the church and came into a tiny lane that the girls had never seen before. It was part of the old village, hidden away between the houses, a memory of long ago when there had been fields and trees, and the mist that still straddled Fog Lane in autumn and winter had come from the low lying fields now succeeded by rows of houses.

Anita caught a glimpse of the lane and the name at the end of it. Paradise Meadow.

The meadow was small, hardly big enough to keep a pony, but here there was a ruined shed and a five-barred gate and beside the meadow was an old house, tumble-down and decrepit, long ago condemned but for some reason forgotten by the authorities.

The man left the horse and cart for a moment and went inside to light his fire so the gypsy girls slipped out of their hiding place and climbed into the field and hid behind the hedge, shivering in the wicked wind that showered the field with snow, hiding its ugliness.

The man came back. His fingers were clumsy with drink and pulled and tugged at the buckles. He was cold, and he kicked the unresisting pony in temper, wanting to be by his fireside and safe with his bottle of beer again. He had neither wife nor child to comfort him.

At last the pony was free and the man pushed him into the shed, and flung hay at his feet. There was not much and it was not good, but the pony had no choice. He began to eat. The man left the cart and went indoors and the girls watched as the light went on in the decrepit house, and his shadow fell across the thin curtain, as he settled himself in his chair and kicked off his boots before the fire that now blazed, logs burning brightly.

The girls went to the shed. The pony saw them come and lifted his head, and made a tiny whinny of welcome.

'Hush,' Sarina said and rubbed his soft muzzle, and put her arms round his neck. She felt the galls on his back.

'He has harness sores,' she said angrily.

Anita, who had learned the art of healing from her grandmother, felt with her soft fingers.

'No one has taken care of him, ever,' she said passionately. 'That man is wicked. We ought to teach him a lesson.'

'How?' Sarina asked, but Anita did not know.

Romaine had vanished, and only her footsteps showed in the snow. Anita and Sarina waited, and Anita picked out the better pieces of hay and gave them to the pony, and he held his head towards her and rubbed against her dress, to show how much he loved her company and appreciated not being alone.

The slender ghost of a moon slipped up the starry sky and magic spilled over the field. The girls looked at the new-made world, revelling in its beauty. They loved beauty. Their eyes shone, and their small bodies, leaning against the pony, one on either side, warmed him and comforted him, and happiness filled him. He sighed deeply, this time with joy.

Anita took her comb and began to tease it through his mane, her fingers gently pulling at the tangles. He bore it patiently and she whispered to him as Sarina fed him.

'I will make you beautiful. You will be the most beautiful pony in Manchester. Your coat will shine and your mane and tail will be silken and your hooves will be polished and everyone will turn to look at you.'

The moon was brighter now. The stars hung in the sky, far away, overhead, deep in outer space, and the world whirled on, and Sarina took her sharp knife and began to pare the overgrown hooves, her hands so gentle that he scarcely felt them as she brought him comfort. It was a job that she had often done before for her own ponies.

Anita took a dry wisp of hay and began to rub the dust from the pony's coat. She slapped him gently and the clouds of dust flew around them, and she had to stifle a sneeze. She looked anxiously towards the cottage but all was dark. The man had gone to bed and they were safe for the time being.

'No one has ever groomed him,' she said, and she worked to shift the dust and grime and the mud around his legs. He stood patiently, knowing that he would feel better when she had finished.

Romaine came back, drifting on the wind like a snowflake herself, so silent that she made the other girls jump as she spoke.

'There were some apples on the tree in the old orchard, left from autumn,' she whispered. 'The pony can feed on them. And I found some hay in the corner of the farmyard at the end of the lane. No one will miss it.'

The hay was fresh and the pony ate it greedily. He had never fed so well before, not for long ages, longer ago than he could remember, when he was a colt in a green field and the world was new and young and exciting and he could race on smooth turf and chase with his mother.

It was very long ago. He had raced, he remembered, running against other horses on a wide racecourse, when he was only two years old, but his untried muscles rebelled and his legs were strained and the tendons stretched and he had been sold at an auction to a girl who rode him occasionally and kept him in a big field, and then forgot him.

He had been sold again. This time the man bought him, and ever since he had dragged the cart over the streets and come home at night to the tiny field and waited uncomplaining for day to dawn again.

Sometimes children gave him apples and old ladies gave him carrots: sometimes the sun shone and he savoured the warmth and sometimes there was green grass on the verges and the man let him graze, knowing that it saved money in the end. His thoughts slipped through his mind, pictures without words, memories of people's faces, and of voices that spoke to him, and of weather.

'I have one other apple,' Romaine said. 'The Apple of Peace and Freedom that was given to me by my grandmother's grandmother long ago. It keeps fresh for ever.'

Sarina and Anita looked at her.

'Shall I give it to him?' she asked.

Their eyes were troubled. They looked at the pony, at the coat that would never shine again and the hooves that would never trot fast again. He was old and his wind was broken and his legs were knobbly and worn with age and hard work, and he would never know comfort again. Only the lonely desolate field and the man who drank too much and swore too much and who used the whip too often and did not give him food or water, or comfort, or company.

'Give him the apple,' Sarina said, and her hand stroked the soft neck, and the pony wondered why her eyes suddenly filled with tears.

He took the apple, and ate it. Nothing had ever tasted so wonderful. Nothing had ever brought such a feeling of well-being. It was sweet and firm and refreshing and it gave him strange ideas. He lifted his head. Dim memories of far places came to him, of rolling moors where birds called shrill and sweet, and rabbits ran and other ponies cantered, tossing their manes, knowing nothing of roads and carts. The girls, hand in hand, downcast, slipped into the lane, each one kissing the pony as she passed. Silent they turned for home.

The moon was high and the wind was wild, a rushing ecstatic wind that brought with it the scent of the sea, faint and far away, of driftwood and seawrack and the tossing tumbling waves.

Bewitched by the girl who gave him the apple, the pony nosed open the gate. He stared for a moment into the rustling dark. It was so long since freedom had been his. He was not aware that there had been magic in the apple.

He turned into the lane, pushing through brambles and bracken onto a hill. His familiar world had mysteriously vanished and he was in a land beyond time. Uphill to woodland, where the turf was soft and cool and kind, and where there was grass, grass such as he had never tasted, long and green and clean and cool and sweet smelling. He browsed, shadowy beneath a tree, savouring delight.

The grass gave him new energy. He turned and pricked his ears, wary, listening. A rabbit, bounding under his hooves, startled him, but he knew it did not threaten his safety. He sped over the turf, alone in the windy night, trotting faster than he had ever trotted, racing against the wind.

He began to canter. The night and the wind excited him and the soft ground, kind to his hooves, was tempting, so that he fled through the windy dark leaving the town and the seven-acre field and the world's unkindness far behind him.

Somewhere, he did not know where, he was joined by other ponies, long legged, cream coloured, very like himself, manes and tails silken with loving care, and satin coats shining. Now that the girls had groomed him, he was as beautiful as they.

They called to him, and he answered, lifting his voice in joyous ecstasy, a long neighing call that challenged the moon, and brought answering neighs from the ponies running beside him.

They were almost flying, a frieze of cantering beauties, speeding over the moors. They leaped a running brook where water sparkled, gemlike, under the gleaming light, and sped on, tiny divots of turf flashing up behind the urgent hooves.

The pony raced with them, all tiredness forgotten. Now and again one of his companions brushed against him and it was good to feel the warmth and solidity of a companion of his own kind. He could see the splendid creatures all around him, so that there seemed to be hundreds of cream-coloured ponies on the moors.

Then they were dropping towards the sea and the sea smell was a wild excitement and he could remember, how, he did not know, the sting of salt, the surge and roar and thunder of green waters and the wild exotic fury of the rolling waves.

They plunged through a pinewood, the needles kicked up behind them, the birds just awakening, shouting angry calls as the flying bodies sped amongst the trees.

The cliffs were before them, raking into the sky and, beyond them, the world was a-maze with white water as the wind piled the sea to seething fury, and the waves hurled themselves against the rocks and broke high in cascading fountains of white, lacy foam that glittered in the light of the newborn sun.

They were at the edge of the cliffs. They were leaping over, cream ponies dropping from the sky, dropping into the thunder and the foam and fret of the flashing, tumbling sea, bodies arched and beautiful.

The pony did not hesitate. He leaped with his companions, felt the sudden impact of water, the clean coolness, the soothing welcome that told him that, after a lifetime of misery, he had come home.

He was strong, he was powerful, he was gleaming with glory, swimming into the sunrise, calling his kind.

He was power, he was strength, he was beauty, and the years of toil and misery were nothing, and he swam to a life of rousing wonder, of wildness and foam and fret, with his companions, the wild, white horses of the sea.

Far away in a muddy distant field, surrounded by houses that gloomed, and smoke that poured from grimy chimneys, a man whipped his leg and cursed, as he found the body of his dead pony, lying in the mud beside the half-open gate.

LITTLE BLACK AND BIG BLACK

The story of two kittens, orphaned at birth

Life does odd things. One rarely recognises that some small incident may lead, by devious routes, to future involvement. Certainly, when I first saw Pretty, the fluffy white cat that Marian found herself owning by accident, I did not realise that one day she would lead me to spend the most fascinating six weeks that I have ever spent in my life.

I called in on Marian one late October evening, as we both are involved in a fairly large way, with dogs. Not cats. Dogs. I also own two blue point Siamese. Marian stays clear of animals at home, as Sara, the youngest of her three daughters, is violently allergic to them. I cannot even give her a lift in my car, in which my two dogs often travel, without causing her an attack of asthma.

Marian can still work with animals, but for the most part, they can't go home. This is sad, as Sara is as fond of dogs and cats as the rest of the family in spite of her disadvantages, and animals mean as much to all of them as they do to me. Marian always lived with dogs, until Sara was three. She is now nine.

Somehow, the fluffy white cat that sat at the window, day after day, longing to come in, did not seem to affect Sara. And being cat, it was not long before she walked in, and settled in front of the fire. Sara encouraged her. They named her Pretty. She was most exceedingly pretty.

She was in very bad condition; very thin, with terrible ears, almost raw from untreated canker that she had scratched. In no time at all she was adopted, as whoever owned her didn't care a rap. Marian took her to the vet; she was fed vitamins, and she had her ears treated, and startled us all by purring loudly while the painful drops were put in, and the muck was cleaned out of ears that were very sore indeed. She knew that she was being helped, and came to have the treatment of her own free will, sitting on the sideboard daily while she was also brushed and combed, and the tangles were removed from her fur.

She had a very small appetite. Marian wondered if she were really a fit little cat. She was sober, obviously having never belonged in a home, and had never known kind hands on her fur, or a lap to sit in. She very soon discovered that Paula, the oldest, was the owner of a very soft heart, and she also discovered that Paula's bed was a lovely place to sleep, tucked safely against Paula's chin.

I did not see her again for a few weeks, and then she was obviously in kitten. Marian had thought she would have been spayed, but no one had bothered about that either. We all worried as Pretty was most certainly not a fit enough cat to have kittens.

The days passed, and Marian and I were due to go out on some business trip that we had in common. When I called, Pretty was in labour. There was a warm box for her, in the cupboard, by the hot water tank, but she was not having that. She fully intended to have kittens under Marian's bed, and no matter how often she was put back in the box she firmly returned to her chosen place. Marian gave up and we found some old sheeting and covered the carpet and left her.

When we returned there was one kitten. Marian reported that Pretty was lying beside it, cleaning it. I did not go and look. She didn't know me and it's most unfair to thrust a stranger on any animal in the middle of birth or for three weeks afterwards. They may well attack in defence of their young, especially if it is a first litter, and their instincts are strong. They cannot be blamed. Bitches in whelp should never be put with other dogs or bitches as they will guard the growing pups and fight; and will fight like furies once the pups are born, if other dogs come near. Nature takes over, and humans must learn the rules, or they will be bitten. No animal mother likes outsiders near her litter; some will tolerate them; others do not and even those that tolerate suffer stress at being exposed to much outside handling.

So I left Pretty and did not even peep, much as I would have loved to. Marian is not on the telephone and lives four miles from me, and I did not see her for two days, but I did see our vet, as one of the dogs had an injured paw.

I asked about Pretty.

'Didn't you know?' he said. 'I had to operate and do a Caesarian. She wasn't strong enough to stand the shock. In fact, when I did a post mortem I found she had almost no liver. She has been very ill indeed at some time. And never been treated. She couldn't have reared the kittens.'

'Where are they?' I asked.

'Marian has them. They are trying to hand rear them, but they're going to find it tough as they need feeding every two hours, day and night.'

I knew that this would be very tough indeed; the family could cook but they had to go to school; and shopping needed doing; and every two hours meant at least an hour's involvement with milk to mix and feeding to do, and all the household business as well.

I went up to offer to feed during the day while Marian slept and then caught up with household chores. I could shop on my way there. I could also write anywhere; all I needed was a notepad and a pen. I could type later.

All this happened two years ago. I recently discovered the notes I made, and was fascinated by them, remembering those strange weeks, when I left home at 9 a.m. every day, in time to do the 10 a.m. feed; and stayed until four in the afternoon, driving swiftly home to deal with my own chores.

There were three kittens when I arrived; they had been born on March 6th. I first saw them when they were two days old. One of them had been born normally, the other two by Caesarian section. The normally born kitten was larger than the other two. Two were all black, and the third was white, like its mother. It had a birth injury and it was a sick little kitten. They were so small all three could be cupped in one hand.

For the first four days they moved only feebly, scrabbling in the box, huddling towards one another. They squeaked very softly, making a louder noise as feeding time approached. We fed them on a special milk made for kittens, which is obtainable from the vet; and we used a medicine dropper.

This is far from easy as it's possible to get the milk down the wrong way and flood the lungs, so that the baby animals die from drowning in milk. We had to be very careful to hold them correctly, and to put each drop in slowly and watch them swallow. They took one teaspoon at each feed, and for the first four days it was very difficult indeed to get it into them, as they did not seem to understand about feeding.

Then followed the most difficult part of all as no baby animal will empty itself without massage of the tummy by the mother's tongue. This produces both urine and stools, and unless it is done, again death results from retention of waste matter.

The nearest we could get to this was to use warm olive oil, rubbed on very gently with cotton wool. Paper tissues make marvellous nappies for tiny animals, so that all we had to do after that was wait, clean up, and burn. We lined the box with paper tissues too, as by the fourth day they sometimes went by themselves.

It was surprising to see that also by the fourth day the kittens were responding to warmth, and cried when the bottle was moved away from their mouths. By now a sheltie breeder had lent us a tiny feeding bottle, which made life a lot easier.

The kittens were bedded in a cardboard box, kept in front of the hearth. If we moved it, even before they could see, or crawl, they managed to drag themselves to the side nearest to the fire, and always huddled as close to the source of heat as they could get.

By the fifth day we were fascinated to discover they all weighed 3½ ozs, in spite of size differences. By now we were having a lot of trouble with the white kitten. She was difficult to feed, and her movements and reactions were much feebler than the other two. Little Black was now crawling, was a greedy voracious feeder, sucking eagerly, dragging at the teat, and by now too he could navigate, using us as mountains, so that if lifted to our laps, he clambered up us, clawing and squeaking, until he was in the hollow beneath our chins, close against our necks, where he snuggled down and purred. We now found that he cried miserably if he were put back in his box after feeding and emptying, without being cuddled and mothered. Big Black was also climbing us, but he was much more ponderous in movement. The white kitten barely responded.

When I arrived on the sixth day very little writing was done at all, as by now the kittens, though blind, were much stronger and the two blacks were doing press-ups with their back legs. All their movements were a very fast crawl, always towards the source of heat. The white kitten was no longer with them; the other two left her alone, and if she struggled towards them, they at once moved away, isolating her. As they obviously needed a mother figure they had a woollen donkey belonging to Sara in the box, that was about the size of a mother cat. With a hot water bottle under this, they crawled towards it and lay between its legs, trying to suck from it at intervals. The room was about eighty degrees and we were very hot.

By now their claws were visible and were hardening and their whiskers were just appearing as minute tiny bristles. Their teeth showed under the skin of very bright red gums. Mouths and palates were also a very bright red.

On the seventh day the black kittens were feeding well and were obviously progressing. The white kitten was very weak, and worse, her head was swollen. During the afternoon she began to throw herself about, to arch her back and to gasp for air, which was distressing to watch. At one stage she became unconscious. I took her up and warmed and massaged her. Marian was at a school function and I didn't want to present her with a dead kitten when she got back.

The kitten revived and I fed all three. The blacks by now were very greedy and amused me by spreading their toes as babies do while sucking. The little white kitten took ages to feed, and was not at all interested in her bottle.

Marian came home and asked if I would take the white kitten to the vet, who lives near me. We found a doll's shopping basket, lined it with a piece of blanket and a hot water bottle and pads of cotton wool, and I put the little white kitten inside, in a nest, just her small head showing. The injury had obviously abscessed, and her head was misshapen. She was still blind. I put the car heater on and took her to the vet, who drained the abscess and injected her. I fed her at my home, and put her in the airing cupboard until later that evening. When I looked at her she seemed brighter and I fed her again. She took the feed eagerly, and I drove her back to Marian, thinking we had turned the corner and that she would survive.

But after we had fed the two little black kittens, the little white kitten lapsed into unconsciousness, and died. We had tried, but she had no strength and could not stand up to the infection.

We were worried lest she had infected the other pair, but they progressed fast. On the eighth day they began to arch against our hands, using backs and heads, just like adult cats, which looked astonishing with eyes still blind. They also worried us immensely by making a weird clicking noise. We had visions of milk on the lungs, gone down the wrong way, and of bronchial sounds from within, and worried all day. I looked up books when I went home, but found no clues. By now also they made very angry mewing noises when we took out the hot water bottle to renew the hot water, and moved at speed if we turned the box away from the fire, crawling back to the warmest side without any hesitation.

They were endearing after feeding and mothering as they curled together, settling well, sleeping in a twist of legs and heads, close against woollen donkey, who was obviously now their box mother, just as we were their feeding mothers.

The eighth day showed me two obvious kittens; before they might have been anything; just baby animals. Now they were completely cat. They responded strongly to massage, pushing against us and rubbing their heads against our shins. This was necessary for their happiness. If we denied them they were restless, crying and miserable, obviously needing mothering. They greeted us by lifting their heads and nuzzling us, not sucking against us. The clicking was explained, too, as it suddenly changed to an experimental rather rusty and unpractised purr that by the end of the day was a heartfelt throbbing happy sound.

Now we had to arrange our hands so that they could paddle against us with their paws while they were feeding. This kneading movement is common to all small animals, as pushing against the mother releases the milk. It turns in adult dogs to paw giving, which is a memory of early days when pushing against mum released the much-needed milk; now it is a plea for something more adult, like a walk or a biscuit, and there are few breeds that don't paw automatically unless checked. I don't check it; it's part of the dog's make-up, and helps him, as it is a form of communication.

One the eighth day the kittens' ears stood up from their heads, instead of lying flat, and they began to move them, perhaps in response to sounds. They were able to right themselves when they rolled on their backs; before they had just cried when this happened. They were also at last beginning to eliminate without massage, and would crawl away from any wet patches.

On the eleventh day Big Black opened one blue eye and stared at us. The other stayed closed, which looked rather piratical and upset the children who thought he would turn out a freak. We fed them in a darkened room, as strong light is bad for tiny animals. They are always born in the wild in the dark and only brought out when the mother knows they can stand the light. They were becoming almost too active as they could fall out of the box and climb over the fender towards the fire. Fortunately the fender is slippery and they fell off. They now moved faster than we did.

By the twelfth day all four eyes were open and were a very vivid sky blue. Both were very noisy indeed when they were hungry, and were awake a lot of the time and much more active, exploring the box and climbing over donkey. We did not need to massage them, but did have to keep cleaning up the box, as at first they eliminated after every feed, but later this settled to twice a day which was much simpler to cope with.

They took their milk very fast, enjoying it enormously, and by now were having two and a half teaspoons of thick creamy mixture at every feed. They would have taken more, but we had been warned against over-feeding. Obeying the exact instructions on the pack was giving good results, so no risks were taken.

The periods of mothering now needed to be longer or they wouldn't settle at all. They preferred to lie under our chins and arch against us, and purr. They caressed our faces very tenderly with both paws and noses, and then purred loudly and fell asleep, at which point we returned them to the box. We were able to reduce the heat and to feed three-hourly, which made life less frantic.

By the thirteenth day they dropped the night feed, and I was no longer needed. The kittens were very strong by then, moving extremely fast, climbing determinedly when picked up, always going upwards, never down.

They now not only explored the box, but could get under the blankets and explore them, so the hot water bottle had to be very well covered. They climbed over woolly donkey and over each other. They still curled together to sleep, and seemed very peaceful between feeds. On this day, which was my last feeding them, Little Black amused me by discovering he had a tongue, which he put out to clean the milk off his lips, as up to now we had had to do this for him. He now weighed just over six ounces, and sat on the palm of my hand like a midget cat statue.

Their claws were long and sharp and feeding was painful as they gripped the teat tightly, refusing to let go, and when it was eased from them, they anchored their claws in us. It was necessary to prise the teat out of their mouths. Little Black was a bit dim about getting the teat in, but once it was in there were no problems. Big Black was in no doubt; from the time he was lifted from the box, his mouth was open, eagerly seeking for that bottle. As soon as the teat touched him, he clamped on tight, and gulped the feed down. Both made vigorous uninhibited very funny sucking noises.

I visited the kittens as they grew. They became enchanting, knowing us and recognising us, coming to us eagerly for affection, hoping for food. All went extremely well for six weeks, until they were being weaned. And then, for no reason at all, they developed enteritis. There was some about in local cats, and it may have been brought into the house on shoes, or perhaps it was airborne. We will never know. Marian took them to the vet as they had not had any mother's milk to give them protection. Both were in agony, and at that age there was no hope. Their short lives were ended. They had only been part of ours for so little time, yet it seemed endless, and it was surprising how big a gap was left in the house, and how much we all missed their quicksilver movements as they darted around the room, and then climbed us and fell asleep in our laps.

They owed their deaths to neglect, on the part of Pretty's first owners, who didn't care.

THE GUARDIAN

The farm was better guarded than anyone knew, but it took some time to realise it.

The ornamental ducks were the main problem. No one knew why they had chosen to come to the farm, but come they had, and once settled, it became necessary to guard them against the foxes, as, though they were wild birds, they decided to live as farm birds.

There were four of them; handsome birds with their green heads and the bright orange bands around their bodies. The beaches had been dog haunted and each year they lost the babies; so they had come here, where the dogs knew better than to touch the chicks, and where people fed them. It was a far easier life.

Baby had named them. Baby was two, but no one ever called her anything but Baby, as her name of Geraldine didn't seem to suit her. One day she would be renamed, just now she was Baby. She was an energetic noisy morsel, always in the way. She was too fearless for her own good. She herded the ducks and the two big Alsatians and the crossbred collie the dustmen had found on the tip scavenging and brought to the farm. She herded the cats and she herded the three mares, and the stallion.

She would stand in the field and call to the horses, and Majesty reared and waved his forehooves at her, and she laughed. The mares cantered off, manes and tails waving in the wind, and Baby laughed. People called her to come in and come away, but she still laughed.

The biggest duck was Puddle duck, because she preferred the muddy puddles to the clean farm pool. Baby rushed after her, making sure she was in by dusk. She loved Puddle duck more than the others, and was delighted when an uncle found a book about Jemima Puddleduck and gave it to her for Christmas.

The second duck was Quarrel duck, as aggressive as any farmwife, for ever rushing after the other three, apparently berating them. She made more noise than all the others put together and at times Baby could be heard yelling at her to shut up.

The third duck was Muddle duck, who specialised in never quite knowing where the others were. If they were in the big field she was in the little one, frantically calling to them. If they were in the little field she would be searching the reeds at the edge of the pond in the big field, yelling to them to wait, she was coming.

The last duck was Pretty Duck. This was the drake. He

had his own ideas about a duck's life and most of his was spent in the stallion's stable, where interesting bits of food dropped and he could eat twice as much as his wives.

It was the crossbred collie who herded the ducks most as he was fed on duck eggs and he soon discovered that they only appeared in the straw and they only appeared when the ducks were there, so he spent much of his time satisfying his herding instincts by driving the ducks into their box, which was very useful at night, but remarkably annoying during the day as they objected and set up such a noise that everything else in the farmyard yelled too. But the collie cross was sure that once they were in there would be more eggs, and he adored ducks' eggs, hardboiled and cut up on his evening feed. If he found one in the straw he carried it in, his eyes hopefully saying 'Now?'

Between the dog and Baby the ducks led quite a busy life, but they led an even busier life when the mares and the stallion were out, as the mares were curious about these creatures that came to the pool and swam there, unafraid.

Susie, the Shetland, would stand in the water and try to shift them out on to the land, sure water was bad for ducks. Queen, the big old mare who had long been retired from breeding, took an even more active interest, perhaps missing the foals she had mothered so busily and wishing she could mother these creatures. She was even more interested when Quarrel duck managed to foil the collie cross and hide her eggs and hatch out seven fluffy ducklings. Ducklings, Susie was sure, should not swim, and she haunted the pond edge, trying to keep them away.

Numa, who was in foal to Majesty, was too busy preparing for the birth to bother about ducks. She spent most of her time gazing with soulful eyes into nothing, thinking perhaps of the new life to come. It would be her third foal and she adored her babies, driving herself mad by her relentless need to keep them safe from all kinds of imaginary and real disasters, so that she chased endlessly after the babies, keeping them away from the other mares, from the fence and even once from a large fuzzy caterpillar that the foal was eyeing with enormous interest as it crept along the ground. Numa nearly had a nervous breakdown over that.

Majesty ignored the ducks, he was far too proud for such creatures.

There was one other creature with enormous interest in the ducks and that was the fox that hunted in the coppice. Night after night he stalked the farm, his mouth watering as he smelled duck, but their box was fox-proof and he could not break in. He took to lying in the bushes, watching. One day he might find one of them alone; and he might make a quick sortie and duck tasted good.

The adults on the farm were always busy. There were the horses to muck out as they were stabled at night; the yard to hose down, the feed to give and they needed grooming; they needed the attentions of the blacksmith and sometimes of the vet, and there were also the goats and the cows to be milked; and the hens to clean out and the eggs to collect and the geese to guard against as they had a habit of suddenly flying at anyone unwary.

Baby stood her ground and yelled at them but others were not so confident.

All that summer the fox was aware of the busy life of the farm and of Baby in particular whom nobody could ever ignore. It was a wonder, said her mother in irritation, that she didn't end up in the pond with the ducks, drowned. It was a wonder, said her father, that she didn't end up in the baler or the milk churn, or under the tractor. She moved like quicksilver, and was for ever racing from place to place. It was a wonder, said the man who looked after the horses, that she wasn't brained, the way she stood among them when they were racing around the field; Majesty often looked as if he were within an ace of trampling right over her but somehow, even in the maddest moments, he never did.

Majesty was aware of the fox and of fox smell and he didn't like it. He stood at the fence, his sensitive ears moving forwards and backwards, his large eyes trying to make out what creature lay in the bushes. Sometimes he called to the mares. Numa, the least adventurous and the most preoccupied, never answered, but Queen came and stood beside him, trying to see what he was seeing, but devoid now of enough smell to mark that it was fox. Susie, aware of the sharp and musky tang, reared and pranced, and those on the farm wondered what had set her off. She was a skittish animal, not yet two and as yet only half broken.

Baby, living in her own world, continued to herd the ducks and try to drive the horses home at night, and to command the dogs, sending them to their beds, or to the barn or telling them they were bad so that they remained in a continuous state of confusion, as she was totally unpredictable and also usually wrong.

'Bad Spot,' she would yell at the collie cross, asleep in the sun, so that he woke up and tried desperately to work out what he was doing wrong and tried to find another place where he wouldn't be bad, but Baby would follow him and tell him off, so that in the end he took to creeping behind the stallion's manger in the dark where she never thought of looking for him.

One sunny summer day, the horses were out in the big field, and the ducks were on the pond. The family had gone out for the day, except for the man who looked after the horses. He had groomed the stallion and put him in the field, and was sitting in the sunlight on the edge of the little stone wall, eating his butty, thinking of nothing, when he heard a commotion in the field.

He was too far away to do a thing about it, and could only shout, but the wind was strong and his words were blown away.

Quarrel duck had come out of the pond on the side away from the horses, and had begun to make her way steadily round the verge. The fox had seen his chance. He raced across, and sprang and Quarrel Duck was caught in his strong jaws. The noise he made drowned every other noise on the farm.

Majesty turned his head.

The fox was speeding towards the wood, making for the fence, which he could scale like a cat. Quarrel duck, obviously far from dead, was screaming at the top of her very considerable voice, while the other three ducks added their moans and wails to the din.

The fox was several hundred yards from the stallion and going as fast as he could, but Quarrel duck was large and heavy and a remarkably awkward mouthful.

Majesty reared, and roared, a sound that the man had never heard before from any horse's throat.

It was a long way to the fox, but the water was shallow and the stallion splashed through, sending up fountains of sparkling water and also splatters of mud. The fox heard the thunder of hooves behind him and raced on. He was tiring. The duck had been a mistake, and her struggles as she flapped and tried to bat at his face with her beak were beginning to exhaust him.

The speeding hooves came nearer.

The watching man stared.

Majesty reached the fox and turned his back. The powerful hind legs struck the raider in the ribs and sent him rolling. He dropped Quarrel duck, who made off at top speed in an ungainly flying waddle, quacking at the top of her voice. Majesty turned and sped towards the fox and his hooves struck again and again.

The fox crept away to heal his wounds, and to remember that it was unwise to hunt on this farm. Majesty followed Quarrel duck back to the gate; the other ducks joined her, and Majesty nosed them along the ground, pushing them relentlessly towards the man.

He stood and waited, and the man came forward and lifted Quarrel duck, finding that the odd walk had been due to two broken legs. She was also covered in bites. He took her and splinted the legs and injected antibiotic. That night she went to the vet who treated her with wound dressing.

From that day on the ducks had an extra herder, as the stallion would never let them near the field; he checked them and guarded them, and pushed them back towards their box. The drake found his own way of getting to water but all the ducks had to content themselves with the pool, so Baby had to name them all Puddle ducks.

Quarrel duck was unable to follow them but in the long

weeks during which her wounds healed she spent her time in Majesty's stable, and at night refused to be herded back to her own bed. She slept in the manger and there in the morning the collie cross discovered there would always be an egg.

But he knew that it wasn't his, and left it there, as a gift to the stallion that had saved Quarrel duck's life.

People passing often look in wonder at the stallion in the yard, as there, always, in front of him, is a big shelduck, and whenever he stops to rest she folds herself neatly at his hooves and looks up at him, admiration in her eyes.

And she will have nothing whatever now to do with the drake.

THE TAMING OF BABY

Baby had been a problem since the day she was born, when she had yelled in fury at a world that she detested from the moment she opened her eyes.

She was fed, but that never stopped her if she wanted to scream; she was changed, but that had no effect either, and nobody ever realised that the trouble with Baby was that she hated being a baby; she wanted to do things long before she was able, and it remained a major feature of her life.

She struggled to sit up at such an early age that the doctors were astounded. She was trying to walk at an age when most babies are still crawling contentedly. Once she could walk, the world was open to her and she began to climb; she began to run; she began to herd the animals.

Nobody had time for her. Nobody remembered her name was Geraldine; nobody could think of a name that would suit her. Geraldine was certainly wrong.

She lived on a farm, which was part of the trouble as

there are more ways of getting into real trouble on a farm than there are roads to Rome.

The ducks taught her to leave them alone. Muddle duck bit her; so Muddle duck was left in peace. Puddle duck hissed at her, which taught her that Puddle duck too had a mind of her own. Quarrel duck chased her; Quarrel duck had babies and her babies were not going to be exposed to those small ruthless hands, as Baby had no idea of her own strength and she was remarkably sturdy for her age.

Pretty duck, the drake (Baby had named them all) kept well out of her way. When he saw Baby coming plodding down the ramp that led to the stables, he flew over the fence.

The Shetland pony trod on her foot; Baby pestered her all day; offering her food that was suitable, food that was unsuitable, and because she had seen somebody whip a racehorse on television, which she watched far too much, as at least that kept her quiet, she tried to hit Susie with a stick.

Nobody hit Susie with sticks. Certainly not a minute human that stood little higher than a dog.

The big mare huffed at her. Go away, silly little girl. She tossed her head, and because she was very big, Baby did take heed. Majesty, the stallion, was always in his box when Baby was around; or in the big field, and she could not master the latch of the gate, no matter how hard she tried. She had also tried to climb the gate but she fell off and hurt herself, so she did not attempt that again.

She played round the farm machinery although she was told she must not. She ran in front of Joe when he was driving the tractor. Luckily he was a very good driver, but he nearly had a heart attack and Baby laughed at his anger.

She tended to get her own way too often because nobody could cope with the tantrums when she was stopped from doing something she had set her heart on doing.

She might have grown up into a singularly unpleasant girl and an even more unpleasant woman if Grandee hadn't died. Grandee was short for Grande Dame, and she was Baby's father's mother. Grandee and Granda ran a riding stables; a long way from the farm, so Baby barely knew them. Grandee ran the stables; she kept the accounts and booked the lessons and she managed the girls; Granda had nothing to do with the rides. He took in horses for schooling, as he refused to use the word breaking. You don't break a horse; you train it, he said. Who wants an animal without any spirit?

Baby was left with friends and her parents drove to the funeral which was on a bleak and miserable January day. Christmas was still so recent that the town was a blaze of coloured lights as they drove through the night before Grandee was buried.

After the funeral Granda stood looking into the fire.

"I'll have to sell up," he said. "I can't manage this place without your mother. She ran it for me. I can't handle all those girls."

He looked out of the window at the busy yard. Horses had to be fed and exercised, whatever happened to the humans in their lives. A girl was wheeling a barrowload of dirty straw across the yard; a hunter was being saddled for a ride. The rider stood waiting, flicking impatiently at his boots with his whip, having driven forty miles for his day out on a horse, unaware there had been a death in the family.

"You could buy yourself an easily run flat near us," his son suggested, as Granda turned away from the fire and looked out at the busy yard.

"That would be a one way trip to death via Hell," Granda said. "I'll have enough from this place to buy the farm you've always wanted; a big place, with scope to expand; with room for breeding those pedigree Jerseys you've set your heart on; with stables where I can keep the horses sent to me to train. I'm not giving up my life; I'm not sixty yet; may seem old to you, but it doesn't to me. Your mother was unlucky; she was good for a great many years yet; if it hadn't been for that fall five years ago...."

In those days Grandee had ridden with the hounds; she had taken a fence and her horse had slipped in the road and Grandee had been badly hurt; the damage grew worse, and there was nothing anyone could do.

"Just one of those things," Granda said. "I want a place with a house for you and a cottage in the grounds for me; I can be on my own and not have you coming messing about in my life; but I'll be under your nose if things do go wrong and you needn't fuss."

It was almost a year before the move was complete, but at last the family were installed in a big Victorian farm-house that had been well modernized; and Granda was in a cottage that had once belonged to the head man at the stables that had been run there. They had bred horses then; now the Family were all dead, and the place was forlorn and empty when they saw it; a monument to the days when labour had been cheap and men had come to work for love of horses rather than for high wages.

The stables and schooling facilities and the indoor riding school ensured that Granda got an excellent price, and at last the new place was ready; there were byres for the cattle and wonderful pigstys; there were huge barns, and a vast cobbled yard where horses could be led; and there was more room for Baby to get into trouble than she had ever had before.

Baby and Granda had only met briefly. Granda was not too fond of very small children; he liked them older, teach-able and trainable; and he liked them very well behaved.

Nobody could even pretend that Baby was well behaved and after a few weeks in their new home, he realised that not only was she wilful, stubborn, determined, and ex-tremely naughty, but she was also very spoilt as everyone gave into her, or worse, laughed at her naughtiness.

"You're ruining my granddaughter," he said one eve-ning, having been asked to supper. His daughter-in-law was about to comment angrily when her husband stopped her with a gesture.

"How?" he asked.

"She's three; she isn't a baby, and she's going to be called Baby till she's an old woman if you don't change your ways now. She'll act like a baby too for the rest of her life. Nobody is teaching her anything."

"We don't have time; and Geraldine isn't right for her," Baby's mother said.

"What's wrong with Dina? Suits her down to the ground. It's not fair to let her grow up as she is doing; she's in for a very hard time when she starts school as no teacher is going to put up with her tantrums; she winds both of you and all the men round her little finger; she knows who gives in when she screams and who gives in when she smiles. Let me take her in hand. She can help me as I work."

"She'll get herself killed," her mother said.

"She'll get herself killed if someone doesn't show her how dangerous she is about the place; she's always running in front of the tractor; she likes seeing Jack in a rage."

Jack was new to the farm; he hadn't grown up with Baby, as Joe had. He thought her a singularly naughty and unpleasant child. They had left their old farm and their men a hundred miles away.

Next morning Granda walked into Baby's bedroom.

She wanted to be dressed, but everyone was busy.

So she screamed.

He had just worked out that she was nearly four years old.

She stopped screaming and looked at him, and he noticed that for all the noise her eyes were quite dry.

"Time you were dressed young lady," he said.

"Not a young lady. I'm Baby."

"Oh no, you're not. Today's the day you become Dina; a big girl who can dress herself and doesn't scream when things go wrong. You're going to help me today; and I'll make you the best rider in the world."

"Don't want to be a rider. Want Mummy to come and dress me . . . want. . . ." the yells began again.

Granda picked his granddaughter out of her bed and put her on top of the high chest of drawers that had belonged to his grandmother. She was so amazed that she stared at him. There was no way she could get down without jumping and hurting herself.

"You can stay there till you stop screaming, and promise

to dress yourself," he said, and sat in the chair by the window and picked up a book that lay on the floor. Baby's room looked a little as if the tide had flowed in and left it littered with flotsam.

Baby sat.

Granda sat.

Baby began to cry; this time with genuine tears and small sobs, but Granda went on reading. He had spent a great deal of his life with horses that behaved like his granddaughter; he could take any villain and turn him into a good animal, and he thought it high time this small piece of human being was trained to behave as a small girl should. He didn't much like her as she was; and he didn't want a granddaughter whom he disliked.

The sobs went on, but more softly.

Granda looked at his watch. She had been sitting up on the chest for over half an hour. He smiled to himself; if he could tame her she was going to be a woman well worth knowing; something like his wife perhaps. He did not look at her.

He waited. He had learned to wait; horses did not allow impatience. If you were impatient, you regretted it, and today he had left free, as he had thought he might have trouble. Nobody had ever tried to discipline this morsel before.

"Dina will get dressed now," a very small voice said behind him.

"I will get dressed," Granda corrected her, as he lifted her down. He was amused to see that she knew perfectly well how to dress herself, although her mother was summoned every morning to do it for her. Only her sandal buckles defeated her, and they were stiff.

"Do them up," she said, thrusting a small foot at him.

"Please," he said.

There was a moment's silence, and he picked up the book again, and sat down.

"Please."

They went downstairs together, Dina a little way in front. She said nothing but once turned her head and looked at him, a considering look that reminded him of a bitch he had once had that almost broke his heart. This was a lot of character in a very small frame. He would have to be firm and he would have to be cunning and he would have to be careful.

"I want my breakfast," Dina said.

"Them as wants has to wait," Granda said, using an expression that his own grandfather had used. "We're going to collect the eggs before breakfast."

Dina stamped her foot.

"Want breakfast."

This time Granda lifted her to the top of the hall cupboard and she stared down at him, her face red with rage.

"It's not fair. I hate you," she shouted. "Stupid dog."

Granda looked at her, and quite suddenly realised that few people ever talked to the child. She was repeating the phrases she heard, parrot fashion, whether they were appropriate or not. For a moment he was angry with his son and his daughter-in-law, but then he realised that was unfair; the farm took every waking moment and there were never enough hands to help. Men came and went objecting to the way that animals tied them. No going home if a cow was calving; no going home when a horse was sick; no going home before milking time; and harvest was often done by floodlight in a desperate attempt to beat bad weather that had been forecast, and would come as surely as Monday followed Sunday.

Granda sat reading, and Dina sat on the hall cupboard and watched him. He showed no sign whatever of taking the slightest notice of her.

Ten minutes passed. Granda turned over a page.

"Please can we go and get the eggs?" a small voice asked.

Granda smiled and lifted her down.

"That's my Dina," he said. Dina looked up at him, her face thoughtful. She didn't remember anyone ever using quite that voice on her before. It was a very nice voice. It was the sort of voice that made horses want to do every thing that Granda asked them, but Dina didn't know that.

She put the eggs very carefully into the basket. Granda watched her, without seeming to, realising that this small morsel had never been asked to help before, had had no place in the general scheme of things on the farm, had no sense of belonging to anyone but herself; and that no one had ever tried to make her feel part of the place.

"You've collected more eggs than I have," Granda said truthfully, as he had been deliberately very slow. He sorted out the eggs on the kitchen table. Dina's pile was twice as big as his own.

She watched him wash them.

"Now we'll eat," Granda said. "We'll eat in my house, not yours; it would be nice not to eat my breakfast all alone today. And you can help me get it ready."

He was aware of a small girl looking at him through lowered eyelashes.

"One of your eggs for you, and one of my eggs for me," Granda said, picking up two eggs and leading the way across the farmyard where Pretty duck was sitting in the sun. Muddle duck hissed as Baby passed and Granda heard the sound; she would have to learn better than that. Animals hated being teased.

Breakfast was eaten in silence. Dina wasn't at all sure she liked Granda; he made her do things nobody else made her do. She wanted to go out and annoy Jack; he looked so funny when he got mad. She watched the man pass the window. Granda, who saw a great deal when he chose, said nothing. That was another thing that would have to stop.

"Stable time," he said. "Horses need cleaning out and feeding. You can have the new baby rake I bought yesterday."

Open rebellion, Dina soon realised, would get her nowhere. There were too many high shelves in the stables and Granda seemed to have no compunction at all about putting her into a position that made it impossible for her to do anything at all.

She began to rake, slowly, at a snail pace, having not the least intention of doing anything to help. Granda raked hard; gradually the pile of soiled straw grew higher, and higher, until Dina was marooned in the centre of a great heap of straw.

Granda went outside. There was only one way for her

to escape and that was to start to work properly and shift the straw around her into the little barrow he had given her. Or she could stay there.

He cleaned out the other stalls; and fed the horses, and then came back. The barrow was filled, and Dina was putting the last shovelful into the big barrow.

"That's a wonderful job," Granda said happily. Dina looked up at him. That approving voice again.

"Now Majesty needs his breakfast. Suppose you come and help me fill his hayrack? You can pull out little bits while I carry the bale."

Majesty did not like Dina but he did like hay. His liking for hay overcame his dislike, so that when he thanked Granda with a cheek against the man's cheek, Dina reached up her hand, and very gently stroked the soft neck.

The stallion dipped his head and rubbed against Dina's cheek.

"He'll always do that if you're good to him," Granda said.

The small hand crept into his.

Five minutes later Dina's parents looked in disbelief at their small daughter, running happily along beside her grandfather talking to him earnestly. They went into the stable and came out again with a saddle and bridle and went across to another stable that Dina had never been inside.

"This is Honey," Granda said. "I bought her for you; but I couldn't give her to you until I knew you would be kind...if you are ever cruel or tease her in any way, I'll take her and sell her to a nicer little girl."

Dina looked at him and looked at the pony.

"There isn't a nicer little girl, not anywhere," she said with total conviction and Granda laughed.

He pulled his granddaughter's hair, very gently, and smiled down at her.

"I think you're probably right," he said.

"All she needed was a firm hand," he said later to his son. "You need to show a horse, a dog, and a child, just who is master and then you don't have any trouble at all."

His son had his doubts.

Next morning Granda was wakened by a knock on his front door. He went downstairs, and there stood Dina, dressed, except for sandals. She put them on and thrust her foot at him.

"Please do them up," she said. "I've come to help you with the eggs and with the horses."

She waited and was rewarded by Granda's special voice.

"That's my lovely girl," he said, and watched the slow smile spread over her face, and the light that shone in her eyes as she reached up to kiss him.

STORM

Daniel woke.

There was a full moon shining and a fierce wind blowing, and his room was very dark, but the farmyard outside the window was ablaze with light. He sat up and watched the trees dive past his window and rush back again, flying towards the sky.

The night was alive with excitement. A twig tapped, rat-tat-tat-tat, on the window pane.

It was impossible to stay in bed. Daniel ran to the window and looked out. Lights spilled from the stable window on to the cobbled yard. The wind slammed a door inside the house. The crack made Daniel jump, and Scoot, the sheepdog, barked. He hated wind.

Daniel called, but nobody came.

He went into his parents' room, but their bed was empty. He was all alone in the dark house, and the wind was shouting in the trees and the night was wild, and Daniel wanted company.

He dressed, pulling on his jeans and his jersey over his pyjamas. His parents must be in the stable. It wasn't far away, but he didn't like the dark and empty house, and he couldn't reach the light switches.

The farmhouse was very old. The wooden stairs creaked at every step. Daniel held tight to the bannisters, so that he shouldn't fall. It was a long way down to the kitchen where firelight danced on the walls and flickering shadows played hide and seek with the furniture. He could see the shadows now. He was almost down the stairs.

One of the shadows ran towards him. Daniel stopped, and stared into the darkness. He wanted to cry and he wanted to run.

Then something soft brushed his leg and Daniel gasped. There was a tiny mew. It was only the ginger cat, Sandy Green-Eyes, whose shadow had been thrown on the kitchen wall when he came to find Daniel.

Sandy Green-Eyes was company and walked beside Daniel down the last five stairs and into the warm kitchen and across the firelit floor.

Daniel pushed open the thick wooden door that led into the yard. The wind laughed at him and tried to tear it from his hands and shook the door. He slipped outside and the cat came with him and the door slammed shut behind him. Now he could not get back.

The wind rushed at Daniel, snatching at his dark hair, throwing itself against his cold face, pushing hard against his chest. He had to fight it, all the way across the cobbles, which were slippery and polished with rain that had fallen earlier in the night.

Far away over the fields the church clock struck two. Two o'clock in the middle of the night and he was all alone in the dark farmyard. Sandy Green-Eyes weaved his way round Daniel's legs and purred. He too had been lonely, shut by himself in the kitchen when everyone else was out.

Daniel could not imagine what his parents were doing.

He could see them through the stable window. His father was standing quietly, looking at something that was out of sight. His mother was holding a pail. Steam lifted in the air and wreathed itself round her head so there was hot food in the pail. But why, in the middle of the night? Daniel could smell excitement.

He ran to the stable door and banged on it hard. It opened at once.

"Daniel!" His mother said. She took his hand and led him inside and closed the door behind him shutting out the noisy wind, although they could hear it hurtling round the corners, howling at Scoot, who barked again. Sandy Green-Eyes stalked in with Daniel over the rustling straw, jumped to the top of the hay-bale, and curled himself neatly, legs tucked underneath him, tail tucked round him, eyes watching interestedly.

Daniel held his mother's hand and looked about him. He knew, now, that it was his father who was so excited, and this was the feeling that hung on the air. There was no one else there. Only his father's bay mare, Tsarina, standing on the straw, her head outstretched, her deep brown eyes staring at him from under long black lashes. Daniel loved Tsarina more than he loved Scoot the sheep-dog, more than he loved Sandy Green-Eyes, more than he loved the Jersey cows and the new little pigs that squealed in the sty and fought for food.

"Gently, my Queen," his father said and he stroked the mare's neck. "Gently, my beauty." The mare whinnied and stamped in the straw.

"Very soon now," his mother said. "Tsarina is having a foal."

Daniel held his mother's hand even more tightly. A foal on the farm! A tiny beautiful horse. There had never been a foal. He was used to calves and new little pigs and fluffy yellow chicks. But he'd never even seen a new horse. A foal. A real foal. He wanted to run round the stable and to shout, but he stayed very still, knowing that Tsarina hated noise, even when she was not having a foal.

"Now, my Queen," he heard his father say, and his voice trembled with excitement.

"Can I look?" Daniel whispered.

He crept forward. The little foal was the smallest horse he had ever seen. It was unbelievably tiny. But it was warm and alive and perfect and beautiful, the most wonderful thing in all the world. Daniel stared at it, unable to believe that now there were two animals where there had only been one before, that all by herself, Tsarina had grown this foal safe inside her, in the secret dark where she could guard him until he was strong enough to face the cold and windy world.

The mare turned and looked at her son and her great eyes glowed with pride. She bent her head to lick him clean. The foal flickered one ear and sneezed.

"He's beautiful," Daniel whispered. It was the most wonderful night in all his life.

The mare looked at Daniel and moved to protect her little son. He's mine, her brown eyes said. He's mine, and no other mare has ever had such a splendid son. Look at his delicate head and his shining eyes and his slender legs and his little tuft tail and see how handsome he is. She licked the foal again and he lifted his head and she kissed his small wet nose.

The foal tried to stand.

His legs were new and very wobbly and he fell back into the straw.

"He's hurt. He can't stand up," Daniel cried.

His father laughed.

"He's so new he doesn't know how to stand. Just as a baby doesn't know how to walk. But he'll learn much sooner than a baby. By tomorrow he'll be able to run and jump and no baby can do that for a very long time."

Daniel's father put strong arms round the foal and helped him to stand and reach the mare's udder. The foal could not find the milk at first. It turned its head and tried to suck Daniel's finger.

Daniel laughed.

"That won't feed him," he said and then the foal found the milk and began to drink and the mare rubbed her nose along her son's warm back and watched him with proud eyes.

Daniel's father helped the foal to lie down on the floor. They fed the mare and washed her and gave her clean straw.

"There, now," Daniel's mother said. "Let them sleep."

They slipped quietly outside and Sandy Green-Eyes followed them, hoping for some milk himself when they reached the kitchen.

Daniel had one quick last peep before they shut the

stable door. The mare was lying beside her son, her eyes shining with love. Daniel was too excited to speak. He wanted to think about the little foal.

Far away over the fields the church clock struck three. Three o'clock in the middle of the night and he was still up.

The moon had gone. The wind had dropped and the trees were still. Scoot was asleep, his nose poking out of his kennel. Day would come soon. There was light in the kitchen now, for his mother had pressed the switch. Daniel's father poked the fire and added more wood until it blazed warmly. Sandy Green-Eyes drank his milk and curled up on the hearthrug, purring.

Daniel had a big brown mug filled with hot milk too. He sat on the hearthrug and looked at the flames and saw red fields where tiny foals flickered endlessly, dancing round the hearth. He was very nearly asleep.

"What shall we call the foal, Daniel?" his father asked.

Daniel thought.

He remembered the wind that had roared in the trees so that they dived past his window and rushed back towards the sky.

"We'll call him Storm," he said.

Daniel's mother took him upstairs, where more lights now banished the dark. She helped him take off his jeans and his jersey and tucked him back into bed and kissed him goodnight.

Presently Daniel slept, while his father went out to milk the cows, and worked in the warm milking parlour singing happily to himself. Beyond him, in the stable, Storm curled up close against Tsarina's warm body and slept too.

THE REFUGEES

This story began just before Christmas six years ago. It hasn't ended yet; but another story began two thousand years ago at Christmas, and that too has no ending.

No one knows what the years will bring.

I heard this story at a show, last summer. I travel to shows alone, and as a result talk not only to people I know, but often to people I don't know, perhaps admiring a dog. That way, I hear many stories that others never hear.

I am told about the happy little dog that is now working "C". Four years ago its owner found it fastened down on the railway line, which is why it has only half a tail. There is the little crossbred that does such a good "B" round, found with her two day old pups on the rubbish tip.

There are so many stories, but what is most rewarding is that the stories I hear have such happy endings. There are always the people who take on the dogs, and who give them a life that is beyond anything the dog might have expected.

They rarely come to shows to win. It is odd how often they *do* win. The dog, in its own way, repays them for all they have done, because it is never easy to take on a dog with an unhappy past.

Martin didn't only take on a dog. He took on far more.

You must have seen Martin about; and Sheila, his pretty wife. They come to so many shows, always with a tall, tow-headed boy with a little crossbred dog. An odd little dog with more breeds in him than there are weeds in an untended cabbage patch.

Tonga is qualified now for Championship "C". One day, you may see him at Crufts, and few people who watch him will ever know the story behind the dog.

It's quite a story. Martin told it to me while we were waiting to see Tonga work his run off.

* * *

Tonga belongs to Dannie. Six years ago, Dannie lived with his parents in a little terraced house in a city that everyone knows, where war is a daily hazard; where guns and bombs and booby traps are a way of life but where, if you can, you try to live peacefully with your neighbours, to mind your own business, to survive from day to day, even though there are bullets and barricades, and soldiers and those others who take revenge so often.

Dannie had a mother and a father and an older brother and a younger sister and a year old dog named Tonga. His father was a policeman. It was his brother's birthday. There was to be a party, and because Dannie had wanted to buy Mick a very special book, he had only just that day earned enough money from running errands. It wasn't easy to earn money when you were only eleven.

Dannie went out with Tonga to buy the book. "Don't be long," his mother said, "or you'll miss the fun."

The book shop was several streets away. It took time to choose the book; time to have it wrapped; to pay for it; and to receive just ten pence change. Tonga waited patiently. Where Dannie went, he went, even lying on the floor by Dannie's bed.

Dannie heard the guns on his way home. He stopped and hid; it was never wise to be on the streets when the guns were noisy. Bullets didn't always go where they were meant to go. He heard the explosions too; and the sirens, as police cars and ambulances began to move; and fire engines; and people ran.

Dannie ran too, but Tonga caught his wrist and tried to pull him back. Dannie pulled away, and Tonga sat and howled.

Dannie whistled the dog, and leashed him. He walked, slowly, stopping often, moving like a hunted animal from doorway to doorway until he came to his own street.

He looked at the burning ruins of his house. He crept closer, to hear a neighbour weeping and repeating over and over "Not one of them left alive; Mother of God, not even the dog alive."

Another voice spoke near him: a harsh voice, with no mercy in it, and he knew from that voice that his family had died because his father was a policeman. They would be looking for him, but not if they thought he was dead. He had to go away.

He crept into the doorway of a demolished shop that no one had ever bothered to repair. He knew the door opened. It had been a play place for himself and his friends.

He crouched in the dark and waited.

Night came, but he waited still and Tonga, turned from a happy pet into an animal protecting his master, would not let him move until the streets were totally silent.

Dannie crept out, into the darkness. He stood for a long time looking at the ruins of his home. The fire engines had gone; there was nothing but smouldering ashes. It had been a very big car bomb. It had been right outside his home. There were scraps of tangled metal everywhere.

There were no houses left now on either side of his own. There was nowhere he could go; he did not know who was a friend and who was an enemy.

He would have to take Tonga and find a new home. Perhaps he could go to England: his father had often said jokingly they would go and live in England, in peace. It would be Christmas in three days' time. He had seen the preparations around his home: the tree had been waiting for decorating; the presents for wrapping; the puddings and cake were made.

Dannie crept down the streets, a boy who was afraid that if he were seen, he would be shot. He moved like a hunted animal and Tonga by his side was a wild dog, slinking, an alert dog with a growl in his throat for every stray cat, for every footfall.

There was a patrol of soldiers. Dannie waited until they had gone.

There was a single shot in the dark and a cry like no other cry Dannie had ever heard. He ached with misery. His throat ached and his eyes ached and his body felt as if it had been turned to stone. He was cold, he was hungry, and he was afraid with the kind of fear that no boy ought to know.

He did not want to die. Even though he was alone, with no family left, death was a fearful thing; a step into terror. He shivered and crouched and held the dog close for comfort and Tonga licked his face.

Morning came and Dannie was outside the city. He saw a man go out to his car, put a package on the seat and go into the house again. The man had a home and would find food that night; Dannie was hungry. He took the package from the car and ran. He did not stop until he was well away from the lane, and then he ate, and drank from a stream, and curled up in a thicket and slept, with Tonga clutched against him.

He woke when it was dark. He and Tonga were both hungry.

That night they stayed hungry, but in the morning he began to walk again and found a farm. He took eggs from the hens and he and Tonga fed on eggs and stole milk from a bucket, Tonga using his tongue and Dannie his cupped hands to drink. They learned to move silently and swiftly, and not to be seen.

Next day was the day before Christmas. Dannie was walking wearily along the road when a man stopped him. He was an old man, and beside him was a donkey, its panniers full of peat.

"Where are you going, boy?" the man asked, seeing fear in the boy's eyes; seeing hunger, seeing beyond the moment, with the wisdom of the very old.

"To England," Dannie replied.

"There are people here from England," said the old man. "I am going to a dog show. Come with me; you will find food, and you can help me and I will pay you at the end of the day. People take my picture and the donkey's; many of them. She's a fine donkey."

She was a beautiful donkey. Dannie stroked her nose and Tonga butted his leg jealously. They walked until they came to a great field, where there were more dogs than

Dannie had seen in his life. Large dogs and small dogs; shaggy dogs and close haired dogs; dogs of every colour and of every breed, and the people with them were talking and laughing in a way that people Dannie knew never dared to do.

He had forgotten laughter. Now he heard it on every side.

The old man and his donkey stood and posed for picture after picture. He sent Dannie to buy food and Dannie came back with a mountain of sandwiches. He ate ravenously and shared with Tonga and the old man watched and thought and because he was wise, said nothing.

Dannie watched the dogs in the Breed rings; and then he found the dogs in the Obedience rings and was fascinated. One day, he would teach Tonga to work like that. The C ring in particular was the most wonderful thing he had ever seen.

Such dogs. And some of them were crossbreeds, rather like Tonga.

He went back to the old man, who stood and looked at him and thought.

"It will cost a lot of money to go to England. Does your father know?"

"They're dead; all of them," Dannie said, and fear came back and the old man saw it and knew it and nodded his head.

"Wait with me," he said.

The coaches had come back and were loading up. The old man stood beside them, listening to the people.

"That one," he said at last, "they are going to England. They go for a meal first and then come back here. Wait till I tell you."

Dannie watched the coach being loaded with luggage. The driver shut the hatch and went away. Then the old man opened it and lifted Tonga inside and helped Dannie to curl up among the luggage, to pull a mackintosh over his head, to crouch, very small.

They were just in time. The driver put in a final case, and locked the hatch.

Dannie slept. He was exhausted beyond reason and had

not rested properly for two days. Fear had drained him of energy, and grief that he didn't recognise at first as grief. Everything had happened so fast.

He slept until the hatch opened and the driver began to unload. He waited his moment and slipped out, and found himself on the edge of the docks, a great ship behind him. No one noticed him. He straightened his clothes, and took hold of Tonga's leash and joined the queue of slowly moving people, standing close to a boy of his own age holding the most beautiful pedigree dog.

"Were you at the show?" asked the boy, "I didn't see you."

"I was there," Dannie nodded.

"What did you do? Did your dog win?"

"Not this time," replied Dannie.

"Prince got a first," said the boy proudly, and held out the red card.

It meant very little to Dannie. He was worrying now lest the police find him; perhaps he was an illegal immigrant and they would put him in prison. They did terrible things to people in prison. They said so, on radio and on the TV. His worry was growing so fast that he had to run to catch up. This way, he would be last.

He was out in the street in a strange town. This was England? People spoke in a tongue he had never heard; only a few spoke English and they spoke with an accent that was hard to understand. Dannie slipped along the pavement, his heart thudding so loudly he thought everone would hear.

He didn't know where to go. The shops were shut and the town was dark. There were lights in houses and undrawn curtains and people eating and babies playing and the Christmas baubles were glittering bright.

He was hungry. Tonga whimpered; he had not been properly fed for almost three days.

Tomorrow was Christmas.

Dannie turned down a side street and saw the lights of a church; inside was the biggest tree he had ever seen, ablaze with lights. There were parcels on the tree; there were flowers on the altar; huge bronze chrysanthemums, bigger than any he had ever seen. A man was busy with the decorations, putting the finishing touches to the tree. A bearded man with a sad face.

Martin and his wife had no children. They could never have children and it was one of the sorrows of their life, because both had wanted children very much. It hurt most at Christmas when other folk bought presents and put up the tree. This tree was for children from the orphanage. At home, there was no tree. There was no child to work for, no son to follow him, no need to buy presents for a child to open in the morning.

Christmas had so little savour without children to enjoy it.

He turned and saw the boy. A ghost of a boy with a white face, shivering, the dog beside him pleading with huge brown eyes. The boy moved forward to speak to him, and fainted.

Martin lifted him and cradled him against his jacket. When Dannie woke he thought for a moment he was safe with his father, and then he knew his father was dead, and the hidden grief spilled over.

Martin heard the story and was appalled.

He took Dannie home, and he and his wife Sheila fed him and fed Tonga, and put Dannie to bed in the spare room that had never known a child before. Martin went to his neighbours and told them about the boy. He came home with clothes for him lent till the shops opened, and with little gifts that other luckier children had offered at once, to this child without a country, without a home, who had arrived so late on Christmas Eve and come to the church where Martin was to preach in the morning. The midnight service had just ended when the boy had walked in.

"Will they lock me up?" Dannie asked at breakfast on Christmas morning.

"No one will ever lock you up," Sheila replied. "You'll live with us, and be our son. For always. We'll fix it; it will be alright. Everything that happens on Christmas Eve happens for the best. And it is a small miracle."

It would take time, for the boy and the dog to learn to live again; to learn to trust. But for this day, Martin and Sheila managed to blank out fear, so that Dannie opened his gifts and the neighbours called to make him welcome and to bring more gifts, and he and Tonga were feted and fed, and treated like royal princes.

In church that day Dannie sang his thanks, the soft clear voice floating on the air, pure and true.

> "Good Christian men rejoice, with heart
> and soul and voice,
> Give ye heed to what we say, news, news,
> news...."

Martin, standing in the pulpit, looked down at his wife. Their Christmas was perfect.

The years passed.

Martin heard of Dannie's desire to teach his dog to work like the dogs he had seen at the show. It would help the boy and would help the dog; it would be a new interest for himself and for Sheila, and so Dannie went to training school with his dog. And Tonga learned and learned fast and so did Dannie.

They learned quickly because of the tie that bound them together, for they had nothing but each other; they fitted in Martin and Sheila's life, and the past was as if it had never been, but it was there, for them both. Tonga could not bear the sound of rifle fire, and nor could Dannie. Dannie never watched the news; and he shivered when he saw a soldier.

I watched him working. Tonga won and Dannie came out of the ring with the red card.

"He has a First," Dannie said, and smiled at Martin. I wondered if Dannie remembered the boy, six years ago, who had first said those words to him; but it was hard to tell with Dannie.

Each year at Christmas he stands down at the docks and watches the boats come in. Martin and Sheila wonder what he is thinking, as he waits by the sea. Tonga sits beside him, both of them immobile. Then Dannie whistles the dog, and runs home, and every year he brings with him a present for Martin and Sheila, a present that he has spent the year making, that he offers with pride.

One day he might be a sculptor: the model dogs stand there, tributes to his skill. Every little dog is Tonga: Tonga playing and Tonga begging; Tonga staying and Tonga retrieving; there are little models of Tonga round the Christmas crib.

"He cares too much for Tonga," Martin said, and I knew what he meant, and there was nothing anyone could do, because it happens to us all. I watched Dannie walking away, Tonga leaping beside him, Martin and Sheila behind him.

Maybe it isn't much of a story: A boy and his dog, a man and a woman without a family and a boy who lost his through war, and the dog that kept him sane through the years—a part of his past and a part of his future, binding them together.

Maybe Dannie will never win Cruft's. Maybe Tonga will not live to make it. No one knows what the years will bring.

This year brought me a card from Dannie with a picture of Tonga, because when he won and qualified Tonga for Championship C I sent him a card. I often see Martin; we talk, and I ask after Dannie and he asks after my dogs, and we part again.

So many dogs; that is just one story.

This Christmas I was driving past Dannie's home and looked through the window. The tree was lighted and Dannie stood beside it, laughing while Martin handed him the presents to hang. Tonga raced round them, barking.

Happy Christmas, I thought to myself as I drove home to my own home and my own tree and a small grandson waiting with excitement bubbling out of him and my own dogs almost as excited as he, although they don't know what Christmas is about.

Or do they?

The stars glitter, the moon shines bright and peace is around us.

In a war torn world, a boy and a dog found a home.

Happy Christmas Tonga. Happy Christmas Dannie; we'll be seeing you around.

A HITCH IN TIME

There never was such a car. It was a dream, a wonder, a speeding bullet, hurtling down the motorway, eating the miles. A monster of perfection.

Johnny, holding the wheel, answering with his whole being to the needs of the engine, knew, for the first time in his life, a satisfaction that was beyond words.

Everything had gone perfectly, without a hitch. His thick lips curved in a momentary smile, and then he settled again to his driving.

Behind him, the precious case held tightly between his legs, was Lew. Lew's hand stroked the case tenderly. Fifty thousand pounds lay between his feet. Money to buy women who now turned away from him. Money to buy luxuries that other men took for granted. His brown eyes glittered.

Beside him, Lennie also nursed dreams. Perhaps Johnny, who bullied and teased him mercilessly, would now be kind. Undersized, insignificant, a butt for every man, Lennie longed to be important.

Johnny sent the car hurling along the roadway. Years of pent anger now found an outlet. The Jaguar snarled on, obedient to the touch of his foot, a careless movement of his hands.

This was power. This was achievement. Johnny, exulting, caught Lennie's frightened eyes in the mirror and grinned again.

The speedometer needle crawled up. One hundred, one

hundred and ten, one hundred and fifteen. The passing fields were a blur. The cars they overtook were a sudden roar, a soft insistent succeeding sound dying away. The Jaguar was alive and responsive as a woman and life was wonderful and Johnny was whistling under his breath and hurtling away from the robbed bank where the cashier lay in a spill of blood and the bank manager nursed an aching head and tried desperately to describe the men who had rushed in and overpowered them.

Beside Johnny, inscrutable as a Buddha, sat Hank. He had arranged the coup. It had gone so smoothly. Old Job never questioned when they brought the Jag to the garage, saying it belonged to a friend who wanted a re-spray job.

Changed from grey to black, with new number plates, and leopard-skin covers over the formerly grey seats, nobody gave the car a second look.

The bank job had been a pushover. Timed to come just after three big customers had deposited a week's takings, they had met with little resistance. Lennie dealt swiftly with the girl cashier who reached for the alarm. Johnny coshed the manager as he raced out of his office.

Within ten minutes they were outside, not into the Jaguar, but into an old inconspicuous Ford that might have belonged to any housewife shopping. Johnny had parked it outside the supermarket and they walked straight through, out of the rear doors to the car park where the Jaguar waited, parcels and a teddy-bear innocent on the back seat.

Johnny drove sedately through the town. Lennie, grinning, held the teddy-bear on his knee. No-one spared them a second glance.

Once they were on the M1 Johnny let go. He was sure all had gone well. Nobody spotted them as they changed cars, the only tricky part of the whole job. The girl couldn't identify them. Not for a day or so, and then they would be well away.

A lorry was ahead of them, passing an old family rattletrap that ambled lazily along in the slow lane. Johnny glanced in the mirror, waited for a second Jaguar to come up fast in the outside lane, and then moved to take his

place, leaving the lorry a mere memory in the distance.

The second Jaguar was driven by a boy of twenty, a bright-haired girl beside him. He grinned, stimulated by a desire to show off the paces of his gleaming beauty. He put his foot down, racing the getaway car, confining it to the outer lane.

Johnny forgot the hold-up and forgot he had to turn off. He was drunk with speed, with the joy of handling such a powerful engine for the first time in his life, with the thrill of challenge. The speedometer needle flicked upwards. They raced headlong, forgetting everything in a blind urge to find out who was master.

Hank, rousing from a half-doze, swore viciously.

'Are you out of your mind?' He glared at Johnny. 'Want to get us taken in for exceeding the seventy mile limit?'

Johnny eased his foot on the accelerator, shame-faced. He fell behind and the driver of the other car, exultant, chased away. The girl waved derisively as they sped on.

Johnny had missed his turning. He cursed. Hank was a stranger and might not notice. Lew and Lennie were too relieved by the more sober speed to watch the turn-offs. He took the next by-road, planning to make his way back, cross country, to the original route.

It was unnerving to turn into narrow lanes. Ditches, full after weeks of rain, gleamed in the late afternoon sun. Hank glanced at his watch. Soon be dark. The clocks had just been put back an hour.

The lane twisted. Johnny made a racing change, unaware that round the corner lay disaster.

The altered hour meant trouble on the farm. In the far field impatient cattle waited, pushing and milling, lowing because their udders were full and uncomfortable. They wanted to be milked.

Old Silver, whose yield bettered that of her sisters by half as much again, was not only aware of discomfort from her brimming milk bag, but was wily, and understood gates.

Farmer Denton did not de-horn his cattle. Soon she had her left horn under the latch. The bar lifted, the gate slid towards her and she eased through, majestic.

The herd followed, black and white bodies packed solid, each beast anxious not to be left alone.

On the heels of the matrons came the skittish yearlings, mischievous, unused to handling by men. Within minutes the lane was seething with cattle as the herd pushed steadily towards the milking parlour.

Johnny took the corner fast, saw the packed backs in the massed shadows under arching trees, and trod on the brakes. Hank hit his head against the windscreen.

Wheels skidded and the Jaguar twisted. Remorselessly, it slid, and one front wing crumpled against the far side of the brimming ditch. The bonnet leaned crazily askew.

'That's torn it,' Johnny said viciously.

Cows surrounded them. Wet noses marked the windows. Horns scraped the immaculate paintwork. Rosy rubbed her rump ecstatically against the offside rear wing. The car lurched and settled deeper.

Lennie, seeing an opportunity sent from heaven, opened the door, grabbed the case, and jumped. He landed in the lane as the other men, shouting, spilled out after him.

Lennie sped towards the main road, wondering if he could grab a lift, quick.

Silver, her curiosity satisfied, lumbered off to the farm, followed by some of the herd. The others, intrigued by strange events, remained behind.

And so did the heifers, frisking free. Polly saw the running man, and trotted towards him, circling and pirouetting. He waved the case in her face and yelled.

Incensed, Polly butted him. He sprawled full length in the mire. The case slid from his grasp. It burst open. Green and blue and brown notes decorated ditch and hedge and trees, tossed by a frisking wind.

The cowman, alerted when Silver galloped happily into the milking parlour, found chaos. Johnny and Lew and Hank were penned by cattle, yelling wildly, hitting blindly at rump and shoulder. Enraged horns angled towards them.

Lennie lay on the ground, tearful, banknotes spilling in the mud. Polly loomed above him, ready to send him sprawling should he again rise.

Dan was a modern cowman. He used machines that needed as much tending as a motor car engine. He serviced the tractor, filled in forms, and applied for subsidies. He had a quick brain.

The dogs were with him, accustomed to helping him. Bett and Rip were sent swiftly, ordered to keep the cattle close-packed and milling. The circling dogs knew how to handle the herd. The three bank robbers were as inexorably penned as if held in an iron maiden.

Turk, the Dobermann Pinscher that kept the farm free from turkey raiders and cattle rustlers, stood guard above Lennie. One look at the snarling dog kept the man quiet, bitterly aware of icy water seeping through his clothes. He wished he had never listened to the others. The piled money beside him spelled bitterness.

Dan raced to the phone, and brought the farmer and two shotguns. These proved unnecessary, as the milling cattle were sufficient guard. The speeding police car almost suffered the same fate as the bandit Jaguar. Dan had forgotten to warn them.

A second car braked savagely. Blue uniformed men leaped out. Laughter burst from them as they took in the scene. The police dogs were not needed. Filthy, bruised, and greatly saddened, the four bank robbers went quietly. Two policemen stayed behind to rescue the loot from lane and ditch and hedge.

'If she hadn't objected to the late milking,' Dan said, grinning, as he patted a broad black and white shoulder, and pushed Daisy out of the way.

'Never thought any good could come out of changing the hour,' Denton said, fetching the last churn.

In the jail the four men brooded. If it hadn't been for those dratted cows.

Silver stretched her neck to reach the greener grass on the other side of the wire. She was blissfully at ease, watching the shadows flung by trees in the moonlight on the angled bonnet of the Jaguar.

Not till the morning papers told their story did Dan and Farmer Denton realise that Silver had earned them one thousand pounds in reward money.

THE ORDEAL

Tom Masters was a mounted policeman. He had a young horse, a most elegant black horse that he had been training for two long years; two years of very hard work as young horses were always afraid; afraid of traffic and afraid of shadows; ready to race, to run, to bolt, knowing nothing; afraid of people. And until they had learned to conquer fear, they could never be taken into crowds.

Crowds were the most frightening things that any horse could face; people who shouted, people who tossed fire crackers, who lit cigarettes with lighters held almost under the sweating animal's nose; people who roared and screamed and cheered; people who shoved and pushed and jostled.

His name was Shadow, because of his sleek blackness.

He had faced every hazard before, one at a time, but this time was different, and as Shadow watched he knew terror. He also knew his master would be displeased if he showed his terror. He nerved himself, stepping delicately, his heart thumping so loudly that the man leading him could hear it.

Other horses were being led along the lane. A young brown mare trembled at a sudden flare and shied. She had failed the test.

A chestnut gelding whinnied and backed away from a suddenly unfurled umbrella. He had failed too. There was no room in a crowd for a panicky horse. Steady boy, steady. Steady boy, steady. The soft voice sounded gently in Shadow's ears. Not to worry. I'm here, I'm here. We're both in this together.

The man's brown hand was comfort.

The man's deep voice was a calming influence. Some of the terror died, but even so, waiting for his turn to be led through the range of horrors, the horse was aware of noise, of the crash of guns, of flash and flare and yell of fury. He was being put to the final test. Nothing he would ever have to face again would be as bad as this.

Tom Masters hated it, but it was necessary. A crowd was a wicked animal, senseless as any wild beast maddened by panic. In a large crowd, anything might happen and his horse must stand there, calm, patient, steady as a rock, never flinching, never rearing, never running, never trampling. The police horse had to be sheer perfection, totally controlled.

Shadow listened to the noise and trembled. He wanted to turn and run, to fly from the field, to allow fear its head.

'Steady, boy, steady,' said Tom, holding him, seeing the trembling body, feeling pity that he dared not show.

Shadow was brutally aware of the noise; of the frost on the rimed grass, grey in the January sun. A thin snow slatted down, the granules so hard that they pattered on brittle stems of long dead dry brown ghosts of summer flowers.

'Steady, boy, steady,' said Tom again, unperturbed by the din, unworried by the swift speeding sound of flying bullets, by the bitter wind that shivered the trees, by the crash and thunder from the heavy guns at the far end of the field.

Three more horses had gone through the ordeal and all had survived, and were now standing at the far side of the shadowy field, where first dark was blurring the hedges and the faces of the men and their uniforms.

'Six.'

The sudden bark of the number made Shadow shudder. He knew his number. It had been his for two years. The sound was as familiar as was the firm but gentle touch of the man beside him.

They stepped forward. Shadow was suddenly blinded by the wet flapping of wet sheets, the horrors he hated most, met in the first few seconds, wrapping themselves round his head and ears, so they clammed against him, clinging tentacles that he wanted to struggle against, but knew he must not.

He plodded on and the clothes line was behind him.

The damp sheets slipped off his back and left him free from clutter. His ears quivered.

'It wasn't so bad,' said Tom, softly.

The snaking line flickered towards him and flashed away. The black horse's heart pounded. He hadn't recognised that this was just an end of rope. Age old fear of reptiles clenched all his muscles so that he bunched to shy, but again Tom's voice was in his ear, steadying him. 'Only a rope, old boy.'

Tom was Shadow's idol. The horse walked on, and the tight muscles relaxed.

The ground lurched, gave way and crumpled with a noise that outdid the bellowing of a thousand demons. Shadow stopped dead and looked wildly for a way of escape but the path behind him was blocked by men who had moved forward to prevent this, the sides were solid and there was no way out.

He had to go on, over the three panels of corrugated iron that clattered and bent and lifted and rattled. His hooves were on grass again, and he paused, wanting to gain his breath and recover from the pain in his chest caused by his panting breathing.

Crash!

The world blew up in his face.

Streams of fire surrounded his head. Brilliant sparks flew skywards, came to earth in a hiss of sound that was more frightening than the fire itself.

'Good lad. On we go.'

A stick struck him, and all at once whips flailed and his tender skin was shuddering away from roughness. A man swerved across his path, shouting and caught him in the neck with a brutal fist. He knew he must endure, that he was being taught to stand against such treatment, but he longed to retaliate, to flash out viciously with his hind legs, to fling his strength into angry challenge.

"Steady, old lad. Steady,' said Tom. The soft voice was welcome.

Drums beat. Rackets clattered. Trumpets blared. Men roared and joined hands and swayed and sang and shouted, imitating a drunken crowd, rioting on a cold afternoon.

They pushed and thrust and fought, they fell at his feet, fell under him, fell against him, surged away and pushed in another direction and the fencing beside him gave way and crashed to the ground, catching the horse on the shoulder.

Beyond was safety. The twilight field and glittering grass, the silent trees moving in familiar shapes, the first thin semblance of a shadowy moon.

A dummy, imitating a dead body, lay on the ground. He stepped over it delicately.

Almost he missed the unseen hurdle, but caught sight of it in time and took off, catlike, from a standing start, clearing it by more than a foot. He landed, shaking, to stand, stockstill, beside Tom.

He was the last. The dreadful noises stopped. Guns and drums and instruments were packed away. The shouting men were his daytime friends, who came into the stables and patted him on the muzzle, rewarding him with carrots, and with apples, and with horse nuts.

'Good lad,' they said. 'Good lad. Good lad.'

The voices were jubilant. None of them liked the test, but it had to be done. Four horses had passed out of six. There would be four newcomers on the strength.

Tom held out a carrot and Shadow dipped his head and took it, mouthing it gently.

'He'll make a wonderful police horse,' the Inspector said.

'He never turned a hair, even with the clothes line and wet washing. He's always hated that.'

He reached out a hand and felt the wetness of sweat on the silken coat.

'Terrified but game.'

He went away, and the horse bent to crop the crackling grass and blew companionably at the man who had helped him through his ordeal.

It was the beginning of a long career, and Tom and Shadow became familiar to everyone who lived in their district. The horse was often afraid when he worked in crowds, but he never forgot his training and he never bolted. Always there was that voice in his ear.

'Steady, lad. Steady.'

And afterwards the warm peace of the steamy stable and the comfortable smell of his companions and a good meal and a long sleep before the day began again with grooming to make him the handsomest horse of them all.

THE CAT AND THE POET

PART 1.

There was no more love.

Love had died on a cold morning in late October and the cat was desolate. There had been love. There had been a home with a fire in the hearth and warm hands to stroke her soft fur and caress her. There had been a lap on which to sit, and a gentle voice that soothed her fears. She had never known the harsh reality outside the house, or been touched by strange fingers.

Her mistress owned two cats before her. The first was crushed beneath the wheels of a car chasing through the midnight lanes. The second was bitten by a rat and died in an agony of terror that the old lady had shared.

'Never again,' she said, and when she brought the beautiful black queen to share her lonely home, she vowed that the cat would not run the risk of a violent death in the cruel world beyond her garden.

No one visited the old lady. Everyone had forgotten her. She had lost her husband more years ago than she could count. She had no children now. Her son had died in the war. Her daughter had died over a year ago, after a long wasting illness, and only she remained, alone in the house that knew no other sound than the creak of woodwork drying in the warmth from the brilliant flames. The cat, fascinated, lay with her paws curled beneath her and her wide eyes watching the light that danced in the dimly lit room.

There was no money to light the house, and little enough to spare for food, but there was always fire to keep the cat and her mistress warm, and fish to eat, and sometimes, a roast chicken.

There was the soft blanket that lined her basket in the room downstairs, and there was the corner of the bed which she always shared, lying quiet, her body tucked into the back of the old lady's knees. When she woke in the morning she walked daintily up the bed and touched the sleeping face with a gentle paw, and watched bright-eyed as her mistress woke and sat up so that she could savour the elegance of the dark body, the shape of the delicate head, and the wide cat eyes, slanting and beautiful, unfathomable as the sunlit secret summer pools in the faraway forests which the old lady had loved when she was a child.

Although no one visited, the old lady did not complain. She was not too poor. There was enough to live on, and there was the cat to keep her company. She was alone, but never lonely, as she watched the cat wonder at the lengthening shadows, or jump to the sill and chatter in rage at the birds beyond the glass, or dance with a feather, twisting and turning, leaping high in the air, to snatch at a glimmer of moonlight, and then lie, relaxed and exhausted, stretched on the hearthrug.

Long ago, when the old lady married, her home had been part of a village street but the village was gone, replaced by an ugly town, and the fields beyond were only memories. Now there were roads asprawl with redbrick houses and traffic roared past her gate. She rarely went out of the walled garden, where the trees grew high and dense around the house, guarding her from prying eyes. She valued her privacy.

The shopkeepers knew of her, but they did not notice her overmuch or remember her well. There were so many old ladies and they bought so little. A brief word was all they spared her. They had no time.

The children peered through the wrought iron gate into the secret fastnesses of the garden. It held the enchantment of hidden places and unlike their own tidy suburban gardens, was a blaze of colour laced with dim green recesses, where there were places for a child to hide alone with his thoughts.

They were afraid to venture inside. The older children laughed and said the old lady was a witch, and the cat was her familiar spirit. That was why she was always alone. Like their elders, they had no time for the folk that life forgot.

No one had time. Men lived in a whirlwind of activity, racing from home to work in their cars, and home again at night, with no time to stop and ponder, no time to think of others, no time to stand under the trees or dream in the meadows. They forgot to look up at the nightbright stars, forgot to ponder on the infinity of space that would have reassured them and reduced their problems to brief unimportance. Other worlds would shine on long after man was nothing but a pathetic memory in the networks of the universe.

The old lady often looked at the stars. She walked in the garden, holding the cat in her arms, and together they savoured the excitement of the wind driving through the tossing branches, of the moon glowing serene and remote far above them, of the rain that fell from massy grey clouds. She knew that time was endless and her part in it ephemeral.

Death, when he came, was kind and took her as she slept. That morning the cat walked up the bed and touched the soft sleeping cheek and it was cold. The blue eyes stared blindly at the ceiling. The gentle veined hands did not move.

The cat could not understand. She was hungry and there was no one to feed her. She was lonely, but her mistress had no love left. She had kittens growing inside her, as her mistress had one friend who knew her, not well, but better than anyone else knew her. The veterinary surgeon who attended the cat when she was ill. He had brought the Tom to visit them, only two weeks before, thinking that kittens would liven the house. The old lady had agreed gaily. Kittens would be fun.

The cat stayed on the bed most of the day. She left once to drink from the dripping tap and came back and tried to rouse the old lady, but there was nothing she could do. She slept in the cold house, and she was very hungry.

Next day the milkman saw that the bottles he had left the morning before had not been taken in and he called the police. The cat hid, terrified, as glass was broken in a window, and crouched silently under the bed, watching the enormous trouser-clad legs that came into the room.

More men came, and when they brought the stretcher to the bedroom she slipped, unseen, out of the room and down the stairs and into the garden away from the noise of their loud voices and the tramp of their heavy feet. She watched from the bushes as they boarded the broken window and sealed the heavy door. She was out in the cold, for ever.

The neighbours did not know that the old lady existed. They could not see over the wall. The children had forgotten her. The police sergeant who told those nearby of the old lady's death was shocked by their lack of interest. They had not visited, had not cared enough to call and see if she were ill, or well, or needed help. They did not even know her name.

'We had no time,' the wives said, shrugging. 'We've our own affairs. There's no time for anything else.'

The sergeant went away, angry. The women felt a brief guilt and then filled their lives with busynesses and no one knew that the cat was in the frost-rimed garden and that there was no one there to feed her, and that her kittens were due in a few weeks time.

She craved love. She needed hands on her fur and a lap to sit in and to be told that she was beautiful. She found mice, but she had never eaten mice before and they made her ill. She caught a bird, but the feathers clung to her mouth and there was so little to eat by the time she had finished. She hungered for fish and chicken, and a taste of liver. She longed for the warmth of the fire. There was a bitter chill in the wind and the nights were frosty and the rain wetted her and burrs left from summer weeds caught in her coat and she had a thorn in her paw and there was no one to remove it.

She cried in the night and those who heard her thought the old lady's ghost had come to haunt the garden and condemn their apathy and passed hastily by. She drank from ice-skinned puddles. She grew gaunt and her fur was harsh and her eyes reflected the colour of the moon and were dark with despair.

She watched men take away the furniture from the house. Everything she had known vanished. The windows were blank and uncurtained, the big vans removed all trace of her life with the old lady and now she knew, with utter certainty, that her mistress was gone for ever.

She left the garden.

She had to find love.

She had to find a home for her kittens.

There was no more love.

There had been love once, but love died with the unpaid bills and the hire purchase agreements and the lack of understanding. It died in sorrow and recrimination, its brightness tarnished.

There had been love.

The man was a writer, to whom words were more precious than jewels. When he wrote the small pleasures of life were enriched and transmuted into fables and dreams. His name was Steven Bligh.

The girl was a fashion model. She was the loveliest creature he had ever seen and he wrote poems to her beauty, poems which enchanted her, as no man had treated her so before.

She was elegant and appealed to his senses. She had wide green eyes and ashgold hair, and slim hands that demanded jewels to emphasise their grace. He admired her perfection, and longed to share his riches with her.

As yet, few men knew his work, and his wealth was not counted in worldly terms. His were the hidden places of the world, where wild creatures came to drink and rare birds flew. His excitement came from the wind on the hill and the shape of trees, and the sound of running water.

He showed her the autumn trees, russet and green and gold, and she thought that a russet coat would suit her, and a dress the colour of the beech trees would enhance her ashgold hair.

He showed her a lake. Sky and trees looked up at them

from the water, a perfection of imagery. A leaping otter flashed in the sun. A bird dived. She leaned forward and saw her reflected face, and noticed that her hair was ruffled by the wind.

She saw nothing but herself.

The poet realised that she had never loved him. She had loved the praise he gave to her beauty. Once he tried to tell her that youth faded, outlines blurred, and blonde hair darkened. She would, one day, look in her mirror and see how time had cheated her, and resent the young beauties who usurped her throne.

She looked at him contemptuously, arrogant with confidence. Her looks would never fade. He said no more, and the months passed. She railed at his lack of money. She needed furs to offset her delicacy, rings for her dainty fingers, jewels to enhance her. He could not give them to her.

She could not understand his need to write. He could earn money in other ways or he could change his style and write stories of passion and war, and become rich. She demanded his attention, yet when he found that words did not flow and mundane worries strangled his imagination, and turned to her for comfort, he could not touch her, lest he marred her hair, or spoiled her make-up, and she had a photographic session in the morning, and she needed sleep.

Without love there was nothing. Yet, somehow, he had to share his pleasures. He was transfixed by the light of the moon on the rustling leaves on a windy night, so that he wove it into a story. He wrote a book about the deer and the autumn forests.

His wife laughed at his stories. There were no women in them. Nobody would buy them.

He began to travel. He needed peace and time to heal the bruises that she inflicted daily on his soul. He walked in northern forests and wrote more of the deer, hidden in their secret places; he sailed upon distant seas and captured the exhilaration of seals diving in deep water; he sat beside Scottish burns and knew the joy of an otter swimming through the misty dawn; he watched a harvest mouse build her nest and saw her playing with her young and knew that even the smallest creatures understood love.

He returned to the house that he had bought for his beautiful wife, a small house hidden away in a London mews. It was always noisy with people, with the beat of modern music, with clamour, and with men who passed the weary hours as best they could, by drinking.

Steven had no wish to emulate those who sought euphoria from a bottle of wine, or oblivion from drugs that destroyed a man's senses, or a moment's gratification from women who left him unfulfilled, more than ever aware of a great lack in his life. He needed completeness. He needed a companion who would understand the power that drove him. He had nothing but the gift of words.

There had been love, but now there was only pain. His wife railed at his need to write, at the tales that he had to tell, at his coldness, his remoteness, his dependence on dreams.

He was not surprised when she left him. The man who took her had money to spend on rich settings for the splendid gem that he had stolen. She left without regret.

Steven's house was empty. No living creature shared his home. He could only give men stories, and bring to those who were caged in cities the splendours of the wilderness that he explored. He could remind men that they shared their heritage with the small creatures of the earth. He wrote so sensitively and so sincerely that his books began to sell in millions and soon after his wife left him he became famous. Yet no one knew his face.

Only his agent and his publisher knew where he lived. He did not care for the trappings of fame. He was too reserved to take part in bookshop signings or literary luncheons. He was afraid of public adulation.

He wanted peace. He had to be left alone to transmute experience into dreams. He rarely wrote poetry now, but poetry crept into his stories, and coloured his descriptions and those who read his writings were enriched, and treasured his books.

He sold the London house.

He found an old thatched cottage hiding in a cherry

orchard at the end of a country lane. He furnished it simply, choosing autumn colours, rich rusts and browns. In front of the vast old hearth he put a golden rug.

No one but his agent and publisher knew where he had gone. He craved solitude. He needed time. He trusted no one with his confidences. He wanted to write.

There was no more love.

Had there ever been love?

He did not know.

The cat cowered against the high brick wall that enclosed the garden, and watched the shadow that the lamplight cast on the pavement before her. She had never roamed beyond the wall. She crouched, ears flat, as a monster with brilliant eyes hurtled towards her, roaring defiance. It was going to end her life. She relaxed briefly as it sped by, intent on other prey than her.

Her paws padded on the hard ground. She was limping. She was desolate and the days were passing. Her kittens were growing and though she might survive in the outside world of wind and rain and ice in the mornings they would not. She did not know that she was having kittens. She only knew that she had a driving urge to find sanctuary for some purpose that at present defeated her. She must find warmth and four walls to shelter her and perhaps, one day, there would be hands on her fur again and a soft voice to soothe away her fears.

She came to a shop doorway. A gigantic cat crouched inside and swore at her. He fluffed his fur until he was immense, towering above her, wicked with hate, threatening her with death if she put a foot on his territory. His was the shop door and the shop beyond it and the dustbins in the yard and he was sharing with nobody.

She ran. She ran from cats that spat at her in the darkness, she ran from the dog that chased her until she was forced to jump to the top of a wall. Jumping was not easy. Her body was heavy and felt strange and she was not yet used to the bulk of the growing kittens that were moving beneath her heart.

She was hungry. There was food in the dustbins in the

backyards of the houses. One bin in particular attracted her, waking memory. She smelled chicken. She stood against the bin and inserted her paw under the lid. As it moved she thrust harder and it fell with a clang that startled her. A window was thrust up, a harsh voice yelled at her, and she retreated under a bush and crouched, trembling, until the echoes died and the night was still.

She crept out. She jumped to the top of the bin and found a chicken carcase. Her weight overbalanced the bin, and it fell and crashed and rolled. She fled with the carcase in her teeth and the window lifted again and a heavy object was flung into darkness.

'Damned cats,' a male voice said and the window slammed shut.

The bones had been used for soup and were almost devoid of meat, but there was enough to revive her. She left the cleaned bones under the hedge and crept out into the street. It was better to travel at night. Although the roaring wheeled monsters that fled by had enormous glowing eyes, when it was dark there were fewer of them. By day they deafened her and appalled her. She was never sure that they would not see her and change direction and fall on her with a snarl of rage, and kill her as she killed the birds and mice that she found on her travels. She could not understand why the people the monsters had swallowed were not afraid. She had never known a motor car.

November was almost gone. There had been one terrifying night, when noises thundered and lights flashed on the air and children raced in the streets and laughed and the night went mad. She found a safe place under a garden shed and closed her eyes and covered them with her paws, shutting out the blinding flares. She grew used to the cracks and bangs. She couldn't bear the searing lights.

Men did strange things and she marvelled at the fires in the gardens. That night was the only night that she slept warm, lying by a dying bonfire. When the ashes were almost cold, she crept into them, sullying her coat, protected from the frost that nipped the air and the leaves and the grass and that hurt her paws, and made her breath a visible plume before her eyes.

She left the garden and she left the town. There were no more bins to raid. She avoided houses. She had visited one, stopping briefly, yearning at the window lit by flames from the fire that glowed in the warm room inside.

A boy saw her, his face a-grin, and grabbed her before she could run. He tied a cord round her neck and hung a can from it, and then he kicked her. His heavy shoes thudded behind her. His idiot laugh rang in her ears.

She found a hole in a fence and crept through and the string caught and broke and she was free of the can, but not of the cord round her neck, though she sat and tried to scratch it off, and then tried to catch it against a twig protruding from a tree trunk, walking backwards, but it would not come.

Rain fell, and the ground froze. She found mice and ate them. She stalked a bird but it evaded her easily and mocked her from a nearby tree and shouted its anger and the other birds picked up the cry and the air was hideous with their din. She cowered away and a crow on a nearby fence called to his brothers and in a moment they were mobbing her, diving at her, wings black against the sky, pecking at her eyes. She backed under the leaves that piled against the roots of the tree and found a hollow and crawled inside and in time the birds forgot. There was no sanctuary even in the woodland.

She was tired. She was cold. She was hungry. Her body was heavy. The kittens moved inside her and a glimmer of knowledge came to her. She must have food and warmth. She found shelter in a decrepit garden shed on an allotment, and rested for two days. Time was growing short. She fed scantily. A small rabbit had died of cold and she gnawed the frozen carcase.

She had to go on.

The water in the pools was icebound and she could not drink. She was too tired to stalk her food, too heavy to pounce. Her foot hurt where the thorn had festered. She dared not go near houses. Other cats would not tolerate her near their homes and she knew she could not fight.

She had to have food.

There was only food near people.

She crossed the stream which was solid ice and her paws ached with coldness. She looked from a hillside on a village street and when the last light had faded, and the moon glowed on the rooftops, she crept down into the first garden.

A dog snarled, almost in her ear.

She fled.

She ran until the streets vanished and she was in a muddy lane. An owl dived at her and she sought shelter in a ditch but that housed a weasel, and she ran again and found herself in a wide field full of strange smells and enormous beasts that were larger than anything she had ever seen before. A cow moved towards her, and she ran again, ran through nettles and through brambles that caught at her fur, dived under a wire fence that tore her back, leaving a bleeding gash as its barbs raked at her tender skin, ran through a cabbage patch and a bed of heather, and came to sit, panting, bleeding and dishevelled outside a wooden door, with high in the wall beside it, a patch of golden light.

She sat in the dark and stared at the glow and knew that her place was here.

PART 2.

When the cat came into his garden Steven had been away for many weeks. He had watched lions stalk in a jungle clearing beneath a searing African sun. He had ventured into a remote place where flights of flamingoes rose from the water, their feathers blushing in the early dawn. He had seen humming birds dart in the branches of strange tropical trees and a lake of reeds clouded vivid yellow with the bodies of a myriad tiny wagtails that flittered in the breeze.

He had tales to tell of men who worked in outlandish places, and of the beasts that filled their lives. He had a stack of blank paper and he had his typewriter and his head was full of ideas, but he could not write a word. He was exhausted. He needed cool hands on his head and a face to touch with a gentle finger. He needed a voice to soothe him, and a presence in the house.

It was a warm house, a comfortable house, where a log fire blazed and the vivid gold rug lay against the brown carpet and the chairs and curtains were sombre rust and soothed his eyes. Yet it was lonely and bleak and empty and quiet, except for the erratic dripping of a faulty tap, the hasty whirr of the little clock, the slither of a log as the fire shifted and flared into new focus and flame danced on the walls.

He sharpened his pencil, and filled his pen and stacked the paper more tidily. He found a new carbon. The words would not come. He switched out the light and stared into the dark. The garden was grey under a grey pall, but a break in the sky showed a fine thin point of light from a faraway star. Remote and ethereal, a world glamourised by distance. The golden edge of the moon glittered on cloud peaks and a tendril of light fingered the lawn, and shone full into the eyes of the cat as she sat watching him.

He moved to the window, wanting to see her close. She was beauty incarnate, elegance and grace. Not even the marred outline of her kittens could hide her breeding. He could not see that her fur was harsh and she needed food. He only knew that she was gazing at him with such intensity that he had to understand, that she was telling him news of vital importance to both of them. Yet she did not move. She sat, imperious, waiting.

He opened the glass door and went into the night. Frost clung to the branches, glittered white against black twigs, silvered the lawn. She rat in a pool of moonlight and he looked down at her and was suddenly angry as he saw where the wire had torn her.

He looked at her unhappily.

'How can I have a cat?' he asked her. 'I am always away. Who would guard you, care for you when I am not here?'

She could not answer him. She moved and he watched as she walked to the open doorway and stood, hind legs bent, wary, looking round the room.

Now he could see that soon, very soon, her kittens would be born. He could not condemn her to the icy bitterness of night. In the morning he would call a vet, and she would have to find somewhere else to give birth. Meanwhile, just for this night, she must have shelter.

The cat was exploring. She needed to know the house, had to be certain that nothing dangerous lurked under the furniture, that the room was safe, and no dog or other beast hid. There was no trace of dog which was a relief to her. The smells were strange. She had been used to the scent of the soap that her mistress used, to the perfume that she wore, and the delicate fragrance that came from the cream that she put on her hands. Perfume had been the old lady's extravagance, her one last vanity.

The man's house smelled of leather and of tobacco and of the harsh masculine soap on his hands. It smelled of woodsmoke, and of ink. There were other smells. She crouched against the wall, legs bent, tail moving, and she wailed.

'Poor puss,' Steven said, but puss did not suit her. 'Poor cat,' he added. Her eyes regarded him, disturbing him. She came slowly towards him, and he watched her. He loved animals.

'I wonder who you are and where you come from,' he said, and went into the tiny kitchen to look for food that a cat might eat. He gave her milk, but she scorned it, and sat by the sink, gazing at the tap until at last he understood. She did not like milk. She drank slowly, savouring the clean coldness. The water in the fields had been frozen and she had drunk nothing for the past two days.

He opened a tin of chicken breasts and warmed them in a pan. He chopped the white meat and put it on a saucer and watched as she sniffed at it daintily, and then touched the fragments with her right front paw, lifting a piece on her claw to investigate more closely. She looked up at him. Very gently he stroked her head. The dark fur was soft. She needed cleaning and brushing, but would she let him groom and tend her? He did not know. He left her feeding and when he looked back she had settled herself comfortably to eat, her body close to the floor, her neck outstretched, her shoulders prominent.

He loved her shape. Steven drew the curtains to shut

out the darkness from which she had materialized, and sat in his big armchair, his feet close to the fire. He had brought a bowl of warm water with him and a bundle of cotton wool. If she came to him he must groom her. He could not bear to see her looking so unkempt, her fur staring, and went to look for an old hairbrush that he had discarded but never thrown away.

When he returned she was sitting on the hearth-rug washing her face with an urgent paw. He had never seen such grace. He watched her, completely absorbed, and was startled when she turned to look at him and then came to him and jumped on to his knees. She was sure he would not harm her and she needed him so badly.

Her body was fragile under his hands. The kittens were moving and he knew that it would not be long before they were born. The thought worried him. He did not know how cats gave birth, whether the young came easily, or with hardship that would call for human help.

He began to sponge the blood from her back and was relieved to see that when the dirt was washed away there was only a long jagged scratch that would heal cleanly. He removed most of the thorn from her foot but the festering paw needed expert attention. He brushed her fur and was astonished when her rich purr throbbed on the quiet air. When he stopped brushing she pushed her head anxiously against his hand, commanding him to continue, and moved herself so that she was more comfortable, and licked the hand that lay across her slim dark paws.

She gazed up at him. The old lady had been fragile, pink and white face and shining white hair, and blue eyes that smiled down at her. She had been small. The man was tall and burly and at first his size had frightened the cat, so that she almost ran away again. But he moved quietly and his brown eyes were kind and the hands that touched her so gently that she knew that she could trust him.

She needed to trust. Besides the monsters in the road with the eyes of shining light there had been the children who ran screaming after her and a man who kicked at her, and the boy who had tied a tin can to her, and another who had shouted at her as she took food meant for his dog from his doorstep, thinking it had been put there for her benefit.

The man stopped brushing her fur. He leaned back against the cushions and lit his pipe. She looked up a him serenely. His thick hair was grey, his face sunburned and rough from shaving, his mouth full-lipped and, at the moment, quirked at the corners as he watched her, a faint smile lightening his sombre face. She had taken possession. She tucked her head into her chest, her paws over her eyes, and slept, and her throat throbbed in a constant small purr. She was warm. She was fed, her fur was dry and she was safe.

The clock hurried on. The fire died, and the man went upstairs, carrying the cat with him. There was a basket chair beside his bed. He found his warmest jersey and put it on the chair and he laid the cat down gently.

She watched him prepare for the night. She watched him climb into bed, and when he darkened the room she jumped lightly down and padded to the window and leaped to the low chair beside it and then to the sill. She saw the familiar darktime world once more shut off by glass, and swished her tail as an owl floated across the frosted grass, calling its moaning plaint as it flew.

The man was asleep. This was a familiar routine. She jumped down and climbed onto his bed and curled against his knees, in the warm and comfortable hollow made by his bent legs. In the morning she would wake him with a gentle paw on his face. She sighed deeply, and settled herself to dream, and the only noise on the air was the faint sound of their mingled breathing, and the sigh from the bedside clock.

It was dark when the cat opened her eyes. The sun had not yet chased night across the horizon. She woke to anxiety, to growing unease, and then to a flare of terror and pain such as she had never known.

The pain twisted and tore at her, it bound her with thongs of fire, it pulled her body apart. When, for a moment, it ceased, she crawled up the bed, and reached out a paw to tap the man on the cheek.

Pain returned. Her judgement was at fault so that he was startled into wakefulness by the searing rake of her claws across his face. Steven was angry. He reached for the light switch and brightened the room and saw her staring up at him, crouched over her twisting muscles, her eyes agonised, begging him for reassurance. She had never known pain like this.

His anger died.

He could not bear it. He caught her against him, holding her, soothing her with his voice, while feelings that he had thought dead flamed into urgent life and he shared her pain with her, sharing each contraction of the muscles that sought to expel her young, wanting to pant with her, to cry with her, and prayed to the God he had long disowned to help her, to relieve her agony, to bring the kittens fast to lessen her ordeal.

He paced the room, watching her, and lifted her in his arms. It was cold and as the first light of dawn flickered on the window pane he saw that the glass was patterned with thick frost where crystals had grown in the night.

He pulled on trousers and jersey over his clothes, carried the cat downstairs and hurriedly set light to the fire, willing it to blaze. Surely warmth would help her, would ease her, would spare her a little of the anguish.

She no longer knew him. Twice her claws raked his hands as he stroked her, but he did not care. He could not bear to see such suffering. She was weak from wandering, she was more than half-starved. She must have had so little to eat, and as he had feared birth was harsh because she was exhausted. If he could find the family that had thrust her into the cold his anger would sear them. He would damn them in the Press. He would crucify them with words. He strode round the room, wanting to help, unable to do anything but watch.

The telephone was on the desk. There must be a vet somewhere near. He dialled for the operator and told her of his plight. The girl could hear the cat's cries, which were frightening him. She promised help fast and found the vet's number. Steven waited, and as he waited, listening to the dialling tone of the telephone ringing in the vet's home, the first kitten was born. Steven looked across the room at it. It was dead.

At last a voice answered the ringing telephone. He explained quickly, and gave his address. The vet was five miles away, near to the town, but he would come as fast as the conditions of the road permitted. Meanwhile all that Steven could do was to hold her and comfort her and make ready a box for her kittens. Line the box with warm blanket and put a hot water bottle beneath the blanket.

He hurried to fulfill his task, boiling water for the bottle and making strong coffee for himself. There was a second kitten now. This time there was a faint movement and he lifted it, marvelling at its minuteness, and placed it in the box that he had lined with his softest jersey, and warmed with a well padded rubber hot water bottle that he had forgotten he possessed.

He replenished his fire. He sat on the hearth-rug beside the cat. He had put a blanket down for her. She was blind and deaf, unaware of anything but the bands of iron that had seized her muscles. A third kitten was born and that too was dead and then at last there was the sound of an engine, of the brakes binding, of footsteps running up the path and before the vet could knock on the door the man had it open.

'Thank God you've come,' he said.

The vet bent to her. The last two kittens dropped from beneath her tail. Two were dead but three were alive. The vet stared at the cat, and in spite of her condition, recognised her.

'Where did she come from?' he asked.

'Out of the night,' the poet answered.

'I know this cat,' the vet answered, and told him of the old lady and the cat that had been intended to have kittens to brighten the old lady's life. And the cat's. He had only learned of the old lady's death two days before when he had called to see if he would be needed soon and been shocked to find the house empty and deserted and to learn that none of the neighbours even knew that the old lady had a cat, let alone that the cat had gone.

'Sixteen miles,' the vet said as he sank the needle into

her skin. The last traces of birth had come away and she was quiet. 'Sixteen miles and she's walked every step of the way,' he frowned. 'Have you brandy?'

The man nodded, and they diluted it with water and dropped it down her throat with a syringe. She was too exhausted to resist. The vet dressed the cut on her back, extracted the thorn from her paw and bathed the wound that it left, and found the cord round her throat, which had bitten into her skin.

He swore.

'I would prefer a world without men,' he said, and when he had cut away the string he held her to him, and she opened her eyes and looked up at him inscrutably, and he tightened his mouth.

'Will she live?' the poet asked.

'God alone can tell,' the vet said harshly.

He left to busy himself with other beasts, many ill through men's ignorance or ininquities. The poet was given droppers to feed the kits with milk, and more instructions than he could remember. He wrote them down. The cat cried to him and he went to her and she stretched out her paws and he lifted her and held her.

He ate his breakfast from a packet of biscuits, not wishing to disturb her. He put her down when she slept and fed the kittens with drops of warm milk, afraid that they too might die. He refilled the hot water bottle.

He watched the clock tick out the slow minutes, and could not settle to anything. He gazed into the frosty garden. He paced the floor, thinking of the old lady who had lived alone and died alone and of the little cat that had been left to face an unknown world that had treated her harshly. She who had been loved and petted and made so welcome.

She must have been as desolate as he. They needed one another and he could give her a home. He need not travel. There were enough pictures stored in his mind to write a dozen books and perhaps, now, he could bring them to life again. She had unlocked the bands that bound his brain, and freed him from loneliness and misery and soul-destroying self-pity and the pain of knowing that love had died. Her love had died too, unable to avoid the unwitting desertion.

He felt a paw tap at his leg. She was awake and had moved from the blanket and come to him. Her eyes stared at him. He picked her up and she nestled on his lap with her head tucked into the warmth beneath his arm. He held her, and looked out into the garden where the frost had melted under a wintry sun and shadows fell beneath the stark wintry trees, and no birds flew.

Was the cat breathing?

He bent, and put his face against her chest. Soft, almost inaudible, he heard the tiny purr, and as he moved, his anxious face lightening, she opened her eyes, and yawned, revealing a minute mouth and curling tongue. She closed her mouth and touched his cheek with a soft paw, as if she were smoothing away the two livid scratches that she made during her moments of terror.

Steven spent an anxious night. He chopped wood so that he could bank the fire high. The cat had recovered well but the kittens were weak. He hoped that they would live. She needed them. He did not want to give them to her yet. The vet had said that she needed time to recover. She was very soundly asleep.

He fed the kittens every hour, with a few drops of warm milk. They moved and breathed and once one of them mewed, very softly, and the cat woke and her ears pricked forwards, but she was exhausted and did not go to them.

Steven dozed in his armchair. He sat and read, but he did not see the words that he read, or make sense of them. He was tired, and he was angry. The cat woke and he fed her again. She was ravenous and ate a whole tin of chicken breasts and asked for more. He would need to buy food for her. He moved to the big comfortable couch and she jumped up, nestling against his knee. He took his pen.

He had an indictment to write, and he wrote it, his words laced with vitriol, as he told the story of an old lady left to die alone and a little cat that was flung into the wintry world, to make her own way, to find her own food, to seek her own place in which to bring her kittens to life. He told how two kittens had died.

By the time he had finished it morning looked through the windows. The cat woke and stretched and purred softly. She sat up, and washed her face.

He brought shreds of chicken and she ate it from his hand. She settled again, her paws neatly beneath her, her body recovering from the soreness of birth. Whenever he fed her she licked his wrist. Her behaviour was rewarding. He could not give her away now.

The vet called when his surgery ended, bringing fish and meat for her, as he had discovered that Steven lived alone and he could not yet leave the cat and go shopping. The vet also brought bread and meat and newspapers, and took away a list when he went.

'I think they will all survive,' he said, and lifted the kittens and put them beside the cat.

She looked at them with interest. She looked up at the vet and he smiled down at her.

'She does not yet know what they are,' he said. 'This is her first litter.'

One of the kittens yawned. The cat moved her paw and touched the tiny body. The blind eyes puzzled her. She licked the small head. The kitten mewed and she knew that this was hers and she began to wash him, holding him down with her paw, grooming his fur, and then relaxing to look at her babies, so incredibly small, so unbelievably alive, so proudly and passionately hers. Her purr dominated the room.

The vet laughed and Steven smiled.

'I know they will live,' the vet said again, and went out, whistling happily, and savoured the sunlit morning that gilded the last leaves that defied winter and clung to the trees in the poet's garden.

The kittens grew and the cat thrived. Steven watched her grow stronger, learning to feed the kits, circling her body round them, cleaning and grooming them when they had done. She carried them upstairs at night, placing them determinedly on his bed, although he had put a basket for her on the chair beside him, thinking they would be safer there. He might roll on one in his sleep.

He began to rediscover cats. They dominated his days, which were full of interest. He was fascinated by the mother cat's behaviour. Nothing would make her change her mind. If she did not wish to be nursed she struggled for freedom. He brushed her when she chose and not when he chose, and only when he bathed and dressed her cuts did she let him have his own way. She carried the kittens down in the morning and put them in the box that he had prepared for them. She hated them to move, and when their eyes opened and they began to roll over one another, and sometimes fall out, she carefully lifted them in again.

Soon both he and the cat were fully occupied. The kittens were growing fast. Their heads were blunter than hers and round-eared, their coats thick and dark and softer than hers. She often lay with their three heads beneath her chin, her eyes wide and brooding.

Steven watched her. Sometimes he forgot to write as he stored new images in his mind, seeing how she stretched to her full length, a gloss burnishing her coat, her healed scars now fur-covered. She curled to hold the kittens with her two front paws while they suckled. They were hers, and love had returned to her world so that she brimmed with it, purring to them, adoring them, playing with them, reproaching them, guarding them. Sometimes she had moments to spare for him, but not often, as she was very busy.

In the evening she lay daydreaming with the kittens sleeping against her and he looked at her half-closed slit-like slanting eyes and wondered what a cat made of the world. She accepted him fully, and she remembered the vet, but she trusted no one else and when his agent visited the cat took the kittens and hid them and herself, and he could not find any trace of them. She did not reappear until the car drove away and the house was quiet again.

His agent had been disappointed but was pleased to see that Steven could laugh again. The house was untidy, with torn paper on the rug where the kittens had chewed the *Daily News* before he could read it. He did not care about news. He rolled the paper into a ball and they chased it and fought each other for the fun of it.

There was a string tied to a chair, and a catnip mouse that the vet had been given by an old lady who made them, and that he had brought as a joke. The two men watched the cat smell at it, and discard it after a brief moment but it delighted the kittens, who took it in turns to carry it around and to lick it until it was sodden. It lay, dirty and disreputable, in the middle of the golden rug.

'When will your book be ready?' his agent asked, and was satisfied when he showed her a stack of completed pages. He could write again, words spilling from him, while the cat relaxed on the hearth-rug and the kittens explored the room.

He was enchanted by the cat family. He watched them tumble over one another in mock battles. He watched the tangle of paws and tails that struggled inextricably when they tried to bite their mother's nose and she rolled to avoid them.

He was amused when they took their first shaky steps and investigated the house watchfully inch by slow inch, starting at the least sound, ears pricked and eyes wide, ready to run to their mother in an instant if they were alarmed. There were so many noises new to a kitten, and they watched suspiciously the first time that they saw Steven strike a match and were fascinated by the flare of the flame and the hiss of his pipe as he sucked at the stem.

The clatter of his typewriter transfixed one of them as it tumbled round the rung of his chair. The sound of water brought tiny heads peeping round the kitchen door, but the plop as he lit the gas sent them away again.

He asked the vet to bring a guard for the fire, lest they burn their tails. The warmth attracted them and they crept into the hearth and stared into the flames that danced so that there were red reflections in the lambent eyes.

They began to explore. There were trouser legs to climb and Steven found that even kitten claws hurt when the kitten assumed that he was a tree and he was wearing nothing but pyjamas.

Games became more interesting, as one kitten lurked

behind a door and jumped out at its brother, who turned to challenge him. Small head butted at small head, pushing to see which was stronger. The cat watched them, ready to interfere if the fight was too rough.

They had lessons to learn. Mice to be caught when they were older and they too might find themselves in a cold cruel world with only themselves to rely on for food. They stalked the cat's tail and grabbed it, and the poet, learning the game, dangled a piece of string and spent his time watching them pounce and catch, and grip.

They stalked their mother and as they approached her her paw flashed out and caught first one and then the other and held him down and washed him clean. Washed every corner and cranny, from his tail to his small mouth and even inside his ears.

They stalked shadows. They stalked dust motes. They stalked ghosts. They explored the inside of the refrigerator, and Steven learned to look carefully before he shut the door. One fell in the wash basin and almost drowned, as he tried to play with the light that flashed on the water through the window above the bath.

Sunlight flickered and moved and would not be caught. Water splashed and was mysteriously evasive. Small paws, treading in mud or ash, left marks that were regarded with absorbed attention. Paper built into tunnels that were explored, leaped at, torn, twisted and broken. Paper made a wonderful noise.

Christmas came. Steven had not intended to open his cards, but the kittens explored them and found ribbons and he took the ribbons and made new and enticing toys, plaiting them and hanging paper balls on them.

His agent came with a Christmas tree, made especially for the cats, and hung with tinsel and paper chains and pingpong balls and catnip mice and the kittens climbed it and knocked the balls to the ground and chased them and the poet and his agent laughed as they watched. The mother cat crept out of her hiding place, but she would not come near.

The kittens made a pattern in his life. Their movements, their games, their sleeping and their waking had all the quality of a moving frieze, an intrinsic beauty that he could neither describe nor define. They were entertaining to watch. Satisfying too as companions, asking nothing but food and warmth, rewarding him with ardent affection.

After dark, when the kittens were sleeping, curled together, and the mother cat settled on his lap and put her paws across his arm to anchor it comfortably so that she could rest her chin, she looked up at him and he looked down at her and there was between them a total silent communion that was far more expressive than words.

When they took the kittens into the shadowy garden, she paced beside him, and he felt she shared his amusement as her sons hunted mice where no mice could ever be, peering with delicate absorption down the hole above the drain, or batting at a bird that was far out of reach, beyond any cat's catching. The cat fascinated him.

He was enchanted, enthralled, bewitched and mesmerised. He knew what the cat was saying, knew when she was sad, or hungry, or lonely, or when the kittens had tired her beyond endurance, growing livelier and friskier daily. He watched her sitting ghostily in the moonlight looking out into the hidden garden and wondered what her wide cat eyes saw there, wondered if she saw visions, or if her only knowledge was of warmth and softness, and food.

She had become part of him. He could no more leave her than he could stop writing and now when he wrote, he wrote of her, and of the world she saw, of the room, seen from her small size, the furniture enormous, put there expressly for her by the man who knew her needs. The world revolved around her.

Soon the kittens were old enough to go away. He did not want to part with them. He watched as they danced after the leaves that blew in the garden and laughed as they jumped in the snow and played and rolled, and enjoyed his evening games with a piece of dangling string, which they leaped to catch, standing on their hind legs, paws upraised, trying to snatch it from him. He could not keep them for ever.

He had promised one to his publisher and two to his

agent, who did not want a lonely cat in her flat while she was away, and at last he agreed that they should go. He shut the cat in his bedroom on the day that his agent came for them. As she put them into the basket she had brought he felt that he had betrayed a trust. He did not want to see her leave. The car drove away, leaving emptiness behind.

He released the cat. She walked round the house, looking for the kittens. She explored behind the chairs and examined the pantry. She went to the door and her remote eyes accused him.

'We cannot keep them for ever,' he said.

She could not rest. Only when she was sure that they were nowhere in the house did she settle by the fire, and even then she ran to the window at the slightest noise, looking into the darkness as she hoped they would return. He should have let her see them go. Then she would not hope.

He felt like a criminal.

That night she did not come upstairs.

He had betrayed her and she would not forgive him.

She had loved again, and she had lost her loves again, and now she would love no one.

There was no more love.

She had none to spare for him.

PART 3.

The house was unbelievably quiet. It was unbelievably empty. It was unbelievably tidy.

No small paws tracked ashes or ink or mud over the carpet. No imperious wails called to Steven to rescue the kittens from the height of a shelf that had been easy to reach by a series of jumps upwards, but that, on looking down, proved to be terrifyingly far above the floor.

No movements chased away the shadows. No enquiring head peered over the top of his typewriter, no paws patted at the tantalising keys. The newspaper lay untorn and unread in perfect neatness, where he had placed it. The two saucers were no longer needed. The string dangled pointlessly. He burned the catnip mouse that he found beneath his bed together with paper balls and the end of a fish tail that had been cached thoughtfully against future starvation.

The cat ignored him. She sat on the sill, watching the garden, her back towards him, reproaching him with every muscle of her body, reproach even in her rigid tail. She waited. They must be outside. She walked to the back door and sat beside it, looking up at the handle, turning her head to fix him with expressionless eyes, willing him to release her so that she might discover what he had done with her sons.

He dared not let her out.

She watched for her opportunity, following close behind him when he went to the door, but he knew her thoughts and was careful to lift her and shut her in the living room. She struggled to get down, spat at him angrily, and once, she scratched him. She would not relent. Surely she would forgive him, would forget the kittens, would turn to him again.

She would not sit on his knee. She slept on the big couch in the living room, curling there in the evening, ignoring him when he spoke to her or stroked her, inviting her to come to him, console herself with his warmth, with the comfort of his soft bed.

He sorrowed with her and longed to comfort her, knowing compassion. She did not understand. Her horizons were too limited. She did not know that the kittens had gone to homes where they would be petted, appreciated, and cared for. They would miss her and each other at first, but they would forget. She too would forget. He could not tell her that. As yet she would not accept his hands on her fur, or his knees as refuge.

He found he could not write. He sat and looked at the useless keys that needed his fingers to bring them to life. Thoughts would not come. He was trying to describe the sunlit summer world that had vanished, trying to recapture the surge and thrust of a sailing boat, trying to turn into poetry the roll and ripple of deep green water, the fleck of foam as the wind took the spray, the curve of a dolphin's back as it arched into the air. He watched dolphins playing with waves, swoop and dive, dive and swoop, black backs leaping cleanly in a dance of delight. What were words? He needed paints to reveal his thoughts, but a brush could not show movement. It could only freeze it forever, in a pose, a turn of a shoulder, a glance from enigmatic eyes. He looked out at the wintry garden and saw the pearly glow in the opalescent sky, and the brilliant sheen of sunshine on lichen, enhancing its colour. He saw the tracery of stark branches against a background of cloud.

Swans flew overhead, calling, white bodies thrusting through the air, white wings moving in an ecstasy of excitement, belling, and the cat woke and ran to the window and looked out and he looked out too and saw them vanish into the misty distance, and saw the heavy umber glow on the horizon that heralded snowfall.

He looked at the wintry desolation. The world was empty. The swans had gone. Snow threatened. Steven had learned to read the sky, to know that when plumed clouds streamed across the blue, the wind would bellow and rage and rock the cottage, and the trees bow in supplication. He knew that when grey clouds hung low on the rooftops, then rain would come, and would not ease for days, and he knew that when the sky was torn and blue patched, the sun would break through and chase away the gloom.

Now he knew that the sulphur glow would deepen and that snow would fall in the night and the lane would be blocked as it had been the year before. He needed food, for himself and the cat, he needed to stock the woodpile, and to buy enough to last for at least a week.

Steven had not been to the town since the kittens were born. The old car was cold and the engine grumbled, but at last it started. He had money enough for a new one now. Perhaps it would be better to change to a model that was reliable. He did not like driving and was not interested in cars, though he admitted their uses.

The bustle and throng of traffic and people worried him. He shopped quickly, anxious to return home. He was uneasy among crowds. Suppose he could not get back. The little cat might starve. He was unusually curt and impatient with girls who had no sense of urgency, who brought him the wrong food, or who muddled his change. They looked up at him, at his rugged face and brown eyes and mass of rough grey hair, and smiled at him, but he did not see. He saw only the silent reproach in the mysterious glance of the cat, and the shape of her, sitting on the window sill, watching for someone who did not come. Urgency seized him. Forboding filled him. He wanted to take the stupid girls and shake them and shake the people in front who dallied and wasted time, and scream at them to hurry.

He visited grocer and greengrocer and butcher. He loaded the car. The sky threatened him. The light changed, brooding and horrible, a deep fiery glow behind the cloud. He prayed that the car would start.

The engine answered his prayer, but as he drove past one lighted shop he noticed the bright covers of gramophone records in the window, and stopped and ran inside and bought a record player and a stack of classical music. He needed sound in the house.

The engine grumbled and pinked and stalled, but desperation taught him patience and he drove carefully, nursing it along. He must buy a better car. His anxiety increased when he reached the end of the lane and flakes were falling white on the windscreen, large heavy wet flakes that clogged the wipers and lay on the bonnet and lay on the ground. He was only just in time.

He had been away all day. He had left the cat food and water, but dish and bowl were now empty. She was watching the car, her ears pricked and eager, having heard the faltering engine as he turned into the lane.

She had been lonely. She had missed him, even though she had been angry with him. Alone she explored the empty house, and watched on the hearth-rug as the fire died to nothingness. He had built it as high as he dared. He had anchored the guard so that she could not move it and she lay close against the mesh and watched warmth flicker and vanish and the flames fade away until there was only a dim red glimmer in the greyness of ash.

She ate the food he had left for her, and drank the

water. Soon he would come. He had never left her before. He did not come. She jumped to the sill, looking out for him, anxious. She was cold and she was hungry and she needed him and she had not realised that it was he whose hands kept the house warm, and without him it was a cheerless place.

She crouched, looking into the silent garden. She had known warmth before and had lost it. She had been locked out into the cold. This time she was locked in. She could not find freedom, or hunt for herself. She began to hunt anxiously round the house. There was no food in any of the rooms. She rubbed against the refrigerator, knowing that food was kept inside. She could not open the door. She jumped to the sink. Water had dripped from the tap and she lapped at the cold metal. There was water in the bath. She lapped that too.

It was cold downstairs. She ran upstairs again and clambered onto the bed and crept under the covers, curling herself warmly, faintly reassured by the familiar scent of the man, of his soap, and his tobacco, and of his body.

She was so alone. She wanted him to come back to her, to lift her, to stroke her, to feed her, to bring warmth to the fire. She needed him. She slept until dusk clouded the outlines in the room and hunger drove her downstairs. She sat on the sill and watched darkness hide the trees, and heard a first owl call faintly, far over the fields, and saw the white flakes drift from the sky, cloaking the ground.

She jumped down when she heard his key in the door. He had come back. Now there would be food and warmth and life in the empty house. She ran to him and startled him with the fervour of her greeting, weaving through his legs, rubbing against his shins, arching her back to his caressing hand, tail rigid, her body pliant and soft against him.

He added logs to the fire and coaxed it to a blaze. The room was icy. The cottage had little warmth when the fires were out. The cat crouched on the rug, staring into the flames, purring loudly. It was the first time that she had purred since her kittens had gone away.

He closed the door and left her to warm herself while

he brought the purchases from the car. By the time he had finished and had chopped a pile of wood, and had garaged the old vehicle, the ground was already masked, and he was covered with a whiteness that shook off and made damp patches on the kitchen floor.

He drew the curtains and islanded the house with light. He opened the sitting room door and the cat came into the kitchen. He filled her water bowl, and she drank greedily and watched as he cooked fish and shared it with her. He was hungry too and he saw from the way she ate that she was ravenous. Fear had sharpened her appetite. Fear of being left alone.

He wondered about her memory, and if she thought in pictures, or in smells, or in feelings. She was mysterious, because there was so much that he could never know. He could never see as she saw, shapes that were unimaginable, because she did not know their purpose, and she could never wonder about the future, or worry about her health, or any of the other million trivial anxieties that bedevilled men.

That night when the chores were finished, he heaped logs on the fire, and brought out the record player. The cat watched. She was interested again in the world about her, and she looked into the wrappings as he opened the box, and peered inside to make sure that nothing lurked in the paper.

Her ears pricked forwards as he put the record on the turntable and she was startled when it began to spin, watching with wide open eyes. The music enthralled her. Her ears were eloquent. The old lady had not listened to music. She had often turned a switch on a box that brought words into the room, although the cat could never find the speakers.

This was different.

Sound filled the air. The man settled in the chair and lit his pipe. The cat listened, and as the soothing harmonies swelled and faded, and rose to new raptures, she jumped to his lap as if she had never rejected him, and lay with her head resting on his tweed-covered arm, secure against him, aware of the smell of his clothes and the sharp tang of tobacco, soothed and lulled by the beautiful noise that came from the spinning disc.

Outside the snow fell, blotting out fields and hedges and lanes.

Inside was deep contentment.

That night the cat returned to her place on Steven's bed, but the room was cold and she slept beneath the top blanket, as close to him as she could curl. She woke to a room that was brilliant with light, reflecting from deep snow. She touched his face with a gentle paw.

He was warm and contented and comfortable and tried to take her in his arms, but she was restless and hungry. She jumped to the floor and then to the sill, and was mystified, because she could not see through the glass. Snow was piled against it, as high as she could stretch.

She exclaimed, startled. She had seen nothing like that before.

The poet yawned, and shivered as he stepped out of bed. He looked outside, over the top of the snow, seeing how deep it lay in the garden, and how it masked the trees and the gate and the hedge and glittered in the sun. It was very cold.

The world beyond their walls had gone. The milkman did not come, but the poet had remembered to buy tinned milk and did not care. The newspapers did not arrive but who needed news? There was no post, but his usual post was only bills and those could wait. He whistled as he made toast and cooked bacon and fried egg, and he put down fish for the cat and watched her eat and thought that life was good.

No one could interrupt and he could write. He would tell a story about a lonely man who found companionship in the small presence of a cat and found assuagement in tending to her needs, and who found forgetfulness when she climbed onto his knee and purred and rubbed her head against his hand.

He would tell of their life together and the darktime world that so fascinated her that she forgot him as she watched bats swing across the moon, and owls hunting the grass, and the shape of the nightingale that delighted him with its song.

Her world lay at his feet as she trod in long grass that to her must have been a jungle. She delighted in flowers, sniffing at them delicately until her dark nose was covered in pollen. She pawed at them, mystified by the sway of the stem.

He lost himself in her world and the fire burned low and she came to remind him that she existed and was hungry and the room was cold. The log basket needed refilling. He took it and went outside.

The door did not quite close behind him. The cat was intrigued by the snow. She made the opening wider with her paw, and went out into the garden. She left deep marks wherever she trod. She patted at a branch and was showered in soft flakes.

She walked to the gate, which Steven had left open the night before because he had been inside the car and it was too cold to bother to go back and shut it. There was a sparrow feeding on berries on the other side of the lane. The snow was so deep that she sank in at every step, but not deep enough to alarm her. Her eyes on the sparrow, she jumped.

She fell. She fell through soft snow into a deep hole that was filled with water. She cried aloud, but Steven was busy with the wood basket, and he did not hear her. He did not know that she had gone from the house until he found the door open and saw the pawmarks that led to the lane.

He ran down the path, sinking deep at every step. The cat was light and she had not sunk so far. He saw the marks in the lane and the hole through which she had fallen and he flung himself down and discovered that she had gone into the ditch, and at that point the ditch widened into a pool. He knew the pool. He called and heard her faint answering cry. He could not reach her.

He tore at the drift with his hands, but the snow slipped back into the hole that he made. He raced, floundering, to the shed, to find a spade. Snow was piled against the door and he kicked it away and pushed with his shoulders, clearing a space. Time had ceased, was dragging on limping feet, time was vital, time was imperative. The cat was in water that was only just above freezing point and when she became cold she would give up struggling and drown.

He had forgotten that the shed door was locked, and it was weeks since he had seen the key as he rarely went into the shed. He did not know where it was. He hurled his shoulder at the wood. The door splintered around the lock. He flung it open, grabbed the spade and ran, cursing the snow that hampered every step and the ice that froze the path that he had trodden, so that twice he fell full length and picked himself up, sobbing with pain as the ground drove the breath from his body.

He attacked the snow with demon impatience, sending it flying, digging until the pool was exposed. Panic seized him. He could not see the cat. He stepped into the water. It was knee deep and bitter cold. He reached down, feeling for her, and he found her, and pulled her up. She had been totally submerged.

He tucked her into his shirt, against his warm body, ignoring the icy sodden fur, the water that seeped into his clothes, the chill that racked him. His feet were numb. How must she be feeling, if she were even alive?

He ran, careful not to slip, praying as he had never prayed before. He needed her. She had given him so much. His wife had not liked animals, and when he was alone he had not had a cat, because he travelled. Now he could not bear the thought of life without her. She had woven herself into his affections. He held her saturated body against him and was bitterly afraid. He hurried indoors.

Steven closed the door of the kitchen, cursing the carelessness that had left it ajar. If she should die, he would have killed her, as surely as if he had put his two hands round her throat and broken her neck. He had no compassion to spare for himself.

He looked at the cat. Her head hung lifeless, and he did not know what to do. He laid her on a big towel on the kitchen table, wrapped it closely round her and began to rub, and tried to revive her by warmth.

It was useless.

He bent his head to look at her. He opened her mouth

and breathed gently, carefully, into her lungs, offering her his breath to revive her, pleading with her to open her eyes and look at him. He breathed, in, and out, slowly, seeing her ribs move.

Her eyes flickered. She gasped and water spilled from her lungs. She moved her legs. He took her to the fire, which was blazing, and flung on more logs and held her, rubbing her dry, rubbing her warm, talking to her, soothing her, comforting her, caressing her with his voice, commanding her to live.

Three towels were sodden long before he had finished. When he had used a fourth the fur closest to her skin was still damp. He rolled her in a warmed blanket and filled a hot water bottle which he put beside her, and brought warm water, sweetened with glucose, for her to lap.

She was shivering and weak. Her movements were feeble and he was afraid. He had welcomed the snow, because it isolated him and now he cursed his isolation. He needed help. Yet help could not come along the deep snow-filled lanes.

The sound of his door knocker startled the silence.

He ran to open the door and found the postman standing on the step.

'I just wondered if you were alright, sir,' he said.

'I need the vet,' Steven answered. 'Could he get through?'

'He can get through from the north end of the lane, but not from the south.' The postman had had to struggle to get down the lane at all that day, but he hated to think of a man living there entirely alone, cut off from humanity. Anything might happen. He might slip and break a leg, or lie ill and no one know. The postman was both perceptive and kind.

'You're phone's down,' he added. 'I'll ring him from the village. Is it the little cat?' He had often seen her sitting on the windowsill. He had a cat himself.

Steven nodded, and on an impulse, invited the man to come and look.

'She don't look good,' the postman said. 'But cats are surprisingly tough,' he added consolingly. 'I'll make sure he gets the message. But I don't know what it's like up his end of the world.'

There was nothing more to be done.

He waited. He fed the cat with a few drops of warm meat extract. He rubbed her again, but he could not stop her shivering. He did not know what the vet could do, but perhaps there was some injection that would make her sleep and ward off the shock. The clock's slow tick maddened him. He moved into the other room.

He did not want to eat. He warmed some soup and drank it, and made a pot of coffee which he forgot until it was stone cold. He watched the cat. She had not moved since he laid her on the rug. He bent to her, to see if she were still alive. She was shivering.

He felt the blanket. That was now damp and he warmed a big rough towel and rolled her in it and held her in his arms, willing her to warmth. Self recriminations tortured him. He had been so careless. How could she know about snow? How could he have been so stupid? He could not bear the thought that she might die.

He sat and watched flame forests in the fireplace, saw the branches of fire flash and flicker, saw leaves grow and trees flare to life and die. He saw a cave, dark and secret, suddenly illuminated, minute and magical, where flame horses were stabled, and when they left their stalls they jumped over hurdles of glowing wood.

He saw a flame world where cats lived. Cats slipping through the light, cats gliding through the trees, cats sitting, watching him with enigmatic eyes. Cats trying to tell him that a bell was ringing. . . . ringing. . . . ringing. . . .

He woke, and saw that the fire was low and he added a log and then realised that there was a thunderous knocking on the front door. He put the cat on a chair. Her eyes watched him. She was alive, but only just alive.

The vet breezed in, stamping his feet and rubbing his hands, removing his fur gloves and his sheepskin coat, vital and enormous in the quiet room, banging his cold hands against his sides, anxious to dispel the fear that hung in the air and that gazed from Steven's eyes.

The vet bent over the cat.

His manner changed. He lifted her gently and put her on the table, listening as Steven told him what had occurred.

'These things happen,' the vet said comfortably, using his voice to soothe the man as he used it to soothe an injured beast. 'Don't blame yourself.'

He gave the cat an injection.

'It's up to her now,' he said, 'I can't do anything more. Keep her warm. Don't let that fire die down tonight. It's wicked outside and these stone walls don't keep out the cold. If I can, I'll call tomorrow. Give her food if she asks for it, but don't force her.'

There was nothing more to say. He doubted if the cat would live, but how could he tell the man?

Steven dozed and woke and slept again. He dreamed uneasy dreams and the fire burned low. He woke to a cold room. He was stiff and his legs ached with weariness.

The cat roused and woke and yowled at him. He knew by the strength of her voice that she was fully recovered. Morning had come. He must have slept for hours. The snow was clearing. He shook off the dream, and returned to the harsh reality of daily living.

The doorbell rang again.

He went to answer it, ready to greet the vet with good news. The cat had recovered completely. She was asking for food.

A stranger stood on his doorstep.

He stared at her.

She was very small, the top of her head barely reaching to his shoulder. Her fur coat matched the cat's coat. Her soft dark hair matched the cat's fur. Her slanting eyes, set in a delicate face, were the eyes of the woman of his dreams.

'Who are you?' he asked.

She laughed, a soft husky laugh.

'I'm your vet's partner. I don't need to ask if your cat's better. Your face told me that when you opened the door. I must make sure she's fully recovered. My partner is operating this morning, which is why he sent me.'

Steven could not take his eyes from the amber skin, the

slender throat, the way she walked. She removed the fur coat. She was wearing a dress that matched his rug. The cat was nowhere to be seen.

He whistled and the cat answered him from the kitchen. They found her sitting by the refrigerator door.

'She is better,' the girl said. 'She's telling you that she's starving. She had a horrible day yesterday and now she wants to forget.'

'So do I,' Steven answered.

He found fish that he had cooked the day before and warmed it and gave it to the cat. He watched her eat, and his face relaxed.

'Do you have a name?' he asked the girl. He had to know.

'I'm Félice Holden,' she said.

'Félice'? he said, staring at her.

'You look as you've seen a ghost', she said. 'My mother was French.'

'Not a ghost,' he answered. 'A vision.'

She looked about her. Steven had been too busy with the cat to clean up the kitchen or to feed. There were dirty coffee cups on the draining board and no plates. She glanced up at him, and saw that he had not shaved, that his clothes were rumpled and his face grey and exhausted. She knew that he lived alone. Her partner had told her. She felt a sudden pity. He looked forlorn, like a lost dog, and she could never resist an animal.

'When did you last eat?' she asked him.

'I don't know. Breakfast yesterday, I think.'

'Go and sit down. I'm not on duty today. I came because my partner was so worried about your cat. I'll cook your breakfast. And then you'd better sleep.' She pushed him into the other room. He was too tired to protest.

The cat had come back to the fire and was warming herself, lying close curled. She stretched her head across his foot, and purred. The kitchen was full of small comforting sounds. Steven had forgotten how it felt to have another living person in his home. He sat, thinking.

Félice brought a plate piled high with bacon and tomatoes and eggs. She made toast and shared his coffee, sitting at his desk to drink. She looked idly at the books on the shelf above his typewriter, and then more closely. There were six copies of his latest book, fresh from the publisher, on the lowest shelf. She reached out her hand.

'I know you're a writer, my partner told me,' she said. 'Are these yours?'

He nodded.

She came to the fire and curled herself on the rug beside the cat. He could not decide which of them was the more decorative.

'Steven Bligh', she said, looking at the title page. 'Steven Bligh——I've known you for years.' She looked up at him, the tilted amber eyes no longer remote, but excited. 'I know how you see the sunset, and I know how you see the dawn. I know the forests you've explored and the flaming lakes and the deep jungle. I know all your books by heart. All I did not know was your face.'

'Is it a disappointment?' he asked.

She shook her head.

'You are just as I have always imagined,' she said.

There was no need for words. She sat beside the cat, completing his home. He did not want her to leave. He watched her, saw the grace with which she moved, the way she put a hand to her cheek to brush away the strands of hair, the way she lowered the lids over her eyes. She was as aloof as the cat, and as beautiful.

'This is a lovely room,' she said, looking about her. 'A peaceful room. I would have chosen these colours myself.'

'Why'? he asked.

'They're the colours of autumn trees. You're like me. You love autumn above all seasons. The colours come into your books.'

'Why are you a vet?' Steven asked. He needed to know about her.

'I understand animals and I have healing hands.' She put a hand on his face. It was cool and gentle and he knew that she spoke the truth.

'I'm afraid of people.' She stared into the flames, seeing visions. 'They're thoughtless and they have cruel tongues, and they say one thing to your face and another behind your back. Animals never do that. If they hate you they tell you so, and you can win them to you by teaching them to trust. So few people understand that. I have always avoided men.'

The cat woke and jumped to Steven's knee.

'You could trust me,' he said.

Félice smiled.

'I know,' she answered. 'I knew I could trust you when I read your first book. And knew it more truly with every book you wrote. I have them all. You think as I think, see as I see. Only, I cannot put my thoughts into words. You do it for me. All my life I have wanted to meet you.'

The sun sparkled on the snow outside the window. A blackbird sat on the topmost branch of the cherry tree beside the gate and sang. A log fell in the grate. The cat purred.

'You love poetry,' she said.

'Yes,' Steven answered. 'I wrote poetry once long ago.'

'I know. Know you write poems in prose.' She looked into the flames. 'You yourself remind me of a poem,' she added thoughtfully.

'Tell me.' He wanted to hear her voice. He did not want her to go. She turned and looked at him, and he knew that she read his mind and understood his need.

'There is all the time in the world,' she said. 'This is the poem.'

There was music in the falling cadences of her voice. The cat opened her eyes to listen.

Alone he rides, alone
The fair and fatal king;
Dark night is all his own,
That strange and solemn thing.

Which are more full of fate;
The stars, or those sad eyes?
Which are more still and great;
Those brows; or the dark skies?

Although his whole heart yearn
In passionate tragedy;
Never was face so stern
With sweet austerity.

'You know too much about me,' Steven said.

'I know you are lonely,' she answered. 'Your books tell me so. I know you love beauty; and you are gentle; and I have never met a man like you before. You are simple, like an animal. And I have a total understanding of all animals.'

'And all men?' he asked her.

She shook her head.

'Only you. I knew that those words would describe you, when I read your books,' she said.

The room was very quiet.

'I did not know you existed,' he said.

It was a cause for wonder, to think that she read the words that he poured onto paper, and to know that she understood the thoughts and feelings that impelled him before they met.

'Do the words suit me, now that you have seen me?' he asked.

'Even more.' she answered.

He looked into the fire, and saw visions and she knew that he was making a poem.

'Tell me your thoughts,' she said softly.

'It's only a beginning, the germ of a poem,' he said. 'As yet it has no form.'

The words came slowly. He was not used to sharing his dreams, face to face. She watched him, intent, listening.

'I dreamed of beauty.
Morning came.
My dream was gone.
I was alone.
My heart was desolate.
A bell rang.
Beauty came.

And sat upon a hearth-rug
And I knew
That if only she would stay
My life would be complete.'

The blackbird's notes filled the room.

She touched his hand with mothlike fingers and he dared not move.

'I must go now. I will come back whenever I have time. I promise.'

He took her hands and looked into her eyes.

She was fragile and delicate and lovelier than the wife who had left him long ago, although the years had already shadowed her eyes and sadness had marked her face.

'I promise,' she repeated.

There was no need for words between them. In time she would come to him, and he would be enriched by her presence. When he left her to travel she would not be lonely or afraid of approaching age. She had her healing, and she would work among the beasts and talk to him of her triumphs and despairs. Together they would watch the dawn and the sunset and marvel at the owl flying across the moonlit forest.

The cat followed them to the door and he lifted the small beast so that she would not go out, but she no longer trusted the snow. She nestled against his shoulder and purred. Félice stood beside him and together they looked at the whiteness that masked the world, hiding hedge and tree and field. The sun cast blue shadows.

Félice walked down the path towards her car. She turned and smiled at him and the blackbird sang a paeon above her. The cat purred.

Steven went indoors and sat down at his typewriter. He could not sleep. He must write.

The cat lay across his knees.

Sunshine flooded the room.

There was love again.

There would always be love.

YOU'RE NOT BRINGING THAT IN HERE!

I've always maintained that there is nothing in the world more rewarding than a well-trained dog.

"All you need to do," I explained to my wife, Jenny, "is to be firm, be consistent, and expect the dog to obey, and he will.

"Make sure he knows who's boss. It's as easy as training children."

Our two small boys came screaming through the hall, looked into the kitchen, where we were enjoying a quiet cup of coffee, and screamed off again.

"Do they have to?" I asked.

"They're being burglar alarms," Jenny said.

A fusillade of "bang-bangs" echoed in my eardrums.

"Now they're being burglars."

My wife is brilliant at interpreting the child mind.

"Couldn't they be quiet burglars and quiet burglar alarms?" I suggested.

It wasn't even worth a reply.

I thought about that dog. I brooded about it. I had always wanted an animal in the house. Nothing was better for boys than a good, big dog to romp with, to take for walks, to care for.

I saw myself walking down the High Street, accompanied by a St. Bernard, or perhaps a Great Dane. The boys walked beside me, the four of us causing heads to turn, and people to stare with admiring glances.

I began to read the advertisements in the Pets for Sale column.

It was surprising how rarely anyone had a pup on offer. I could buy budgerigars by the score, kittens of all varieties. I could have a pony, "guaranteed quiet: 14 hands. Traffic trained."

I could buy an alligator.

The boys would love an alligator, especially if it lived in the bath and prevented them from using it. But I couldn't imagine Jenny being charmed with it. She hates spiders and daddy-long-legs make her scream, and even worms give her the creeps.

Night after night I scanned the column. Then I found my dog.

Year old, house-trained, free to good home. Owner reluctant to part, but going abroad.

I was sure I had a good home. But I did not tell the family of my plans. If nothing came of them, nobody would be disappointed.

I went to the address.

The dog lived in a beautiful detached house, set well back from the road. Trees sheltered the grounds. (No one could call them a mere garden.) A gravelled drive led to an oak-studded front door.

I knocked, diffidently. My Mini looked very small and lonely and out of place parked out there.

A woman, with all the gloss of a fashion model and the expensive clothes to match, opened the door.

"I've come to offer the dog a good home," I said, feeling both stupid and shabby.

Surely she didn't dress like that every day? Pearls and diamond brooch and all?

She led me into a room that would have swallowed the whole of my house. The dog followed us in.

It was a generously made dog, with large, lolloping paws. I had never seen such a make before. It had a hint of Boxer, and a tinge of Alsatian, a taint of Great Dane, a glimpse of Retriever.

"This is Lollo," she said.

It seemed a ridiculous name for a dog.

"Lollo. Good dog," I said.

Lollo looked at me with immense superciliousness and yawned, exhibiting enormous teeth and a cavernous maw.

I wondered if the boys *would* be thrilled. If the dog stood on its hind legs, it would dwarf them.

"I have been so worried," the lovely lady went on in a fluting voice. "Nobody else has answered the ad and we are flying out tomorrow.

"There is the basket, and here are the brushes, and these four plates belong to the dog. Come on, Lollo. On the lead."

The dog stood up, unfolding immense legs. Bemused, I took the lead. Events seemed to be happening faster than I had expected.

"I know you'll be friends," Lollo's ex-owner said, and gave me a vague but captivating smile. She closed the door firmly.

Lollo looked at me and sat down, plainly sure that he was being kidnapped. I coaxed and smoothed, and finally dragged him into the car. He filled the back seat.

The dog might have cost nothing, but I would obviously need a larger car to fit the family in as well.

I drove as far as the gate and heard ominous noises behind me. I turned my head. Lollo had been very sick...

Jenny met me at our gate.

"Dickie's cut his head and Johnny's fallen off the swing," she said, then looked at Lollo who was struggling out of the car. "Have you gone mad?"

It was not a propitious beginning.

"This is our dog," I said.

I avoided her eyes which had the look in them that I knew so well.

She had developed it when I bought a dishwasher at an antique sale. It was a very good dishwasher, but we would have had to build an annex to house it.

At the next auction, it fetched five pounds less than I paid for it.

Jenny had developed that same look when I bought our first car. It was a beautiful car, a period piece, a genuine antique. Unluckily it seldom went farther than the end of the road, and Jenny wanted a car to drive the children to school.

Yes, I knew that look.

"His owners are going abroad and want a good home,"

I said. "The poor dog is missing them."

"The poor dog is a bitch, as any fool can see," Jenny said acidly. "You're old enough to know the difference. She is also about to whelp.

"I don't think she has room there. You'd better do something about it. And clean up that filthy mess. I'm not looking after a brute like that."

"She came from a stately home," I said lamely.

"I don't care if she came from Buckingham Palace. Anyway, they have the sense to have small dogs," Jenny answered, and marched away, her nose held as high as it would go.

I extricated Lollo and cleaned the car.

I took her into the kitchen, where she occupied all of the floor space in front of the fire. She looked immensely unhappy, and so did Jenny.

"It's a most unhygienic-looking beast, and you don't know where it's been," she said. "You don't know what the boys will pick up. And it's probably got fleas."

"Not from a home like that," I said.

Jenny sniffed.

I brought Lollo a bowl of milk and she drank hungrily. I stroked her tentatively. She licked my hand.

"Good dog," I said.

She looked at me soulfully and leaned her head on my arm. I was kneeling beside her. She began to whimper.

"You'd better get the Vet. I'm not acting midwife to a strange dog—I mean bitch," Jenny observed, walking through the kitchen and out again with a jelly and three plates.

I was apparently not going to be fed, either.

"And we haven't any food for her," she called. "Nursing mothers need a special diet. Her owners were clever, weren't they? I should think she costs about four pounds a week to feed.

"You'd better get a part-time job on top of your other one, and earn the money to keep her."

The door slammed. It opened again.

"On second thoughts you'd better resign yourself to

house-keeping and I'll get a job. I'm not staying in the house alone with that monster."

The door slammed a second time. A cup fell off the draining board and smashed on the tiles.

Lollo whined again.

I went to telephone the Vet. He listened, and sighed.

When I went back to the kitchen Lollo had eaten the corner of the rug and started on a chair leg.

"She must be teething," Jenny said caustically, coming back for the sugar bowl. "Try her with one of our best chairs. It will probably taste better."

I fetched Lollo's basket from the car. She climbed inside, and climbed out again and looked at me. There was not really room inside it to give birth to a mouse, let alone a pup or so.

Johnny put his head round the door.

"It's big," he said. He thought hard. "I don't like big dogs. I want a teensy weensy weensy weensy..."

"OK, son, you've made your point," I said hurriedly.

Johnny can go on like that for days.

Dickie came into the kitchen and went out again. Howling.

"I don't like that dog," he sobbed, and I looked away when Jenny came into the kitchen again for the milk.

"Brute," she hissed.

I wasn't sure which of us she was referring to.

The Vet came. At midnight the Vet and I were still supervising the delivery of the puppies. We had, by then, reached eight. By two o'clock we were exhausted, but Lollo was not. There were eleven.

By five in the morning the Vet thought the delivery was complete. He was wrong. The fifteenth pup made its way into the light, and moved its tiny claws and yawned.

"I congratulate you," the Vet said dryly. "You are now the proud owner of eight bitches and eight dogs. And you owe me forty pounds for delivery fees.

"I'll send you a diet sheet. And she needs cod liver oil, and Bemax, and I should supplement her with one of the more nourishing milk producing foods. She's going to need a lot of milk. And meat. And at least two eggs and a pint of milk a day."

He left, yawning.

"Monday morning," he said, as he drove away.

I had forgotten. Jenny had no idea that we now had sixteen dogs in the house and I had to go to work. In just three and a half hours.

Lollo was lying with a bemused expression on her face. And small wonder. Not every dog... I mean bitch... has fifteen pups at one go.

I began to do sums.

Forty pounds to the Vet. And meat bills, and a pint of milk and two eggs a day and all those vitamins.

I didn't know how to face Jenny.

She came into the kitchen at seven o'clock. I was asleep in the chair but her gasp woke me up.

"I hope you're pleased with yourself," she said. "Not everyone manages twelve dogs at one go."

"Sixteen," I said foolishly, and ducked just in time to avoid the dishmop she threw at me.

Lollo, sensing the atmosphere, bayed, then, quite sure I was being wantonly attacked, growled.

"That does it," Jenny said. "That ferocious brute goes... now."

"I can't turn her out in that condition," I said. "Who on earth would want her?"

"The R.S.P.C.A. Or the Vet. Or advertise. We can't keep her. We need a bigger house. And a bigger car. Just for that."

Johnny crept into the kitchen.

"She has babies," he said, ecstatic. And put out a hand.

Lollo growled.

"Get rid of that dog... I mean bitch," Jenny shouted, grabbing Johnny and erupting from the kitchen.

She put her head inside the door. "I'm not speaking to you until you do."

It was time to go to work.

I looked at Lollo and she looked at me. I wished I had

known what I was taking on when I answered that advertisement.

I thought of little else all day.

I made several mistakes in my calculations, and I gave Mr Jenson, who is one of the Bank's most important customers, ten pounds too little when he came to cash a cheque.

All I could think of was Lollo, and Jenny there on her own. I expected the telephone to ring all morning.

By afternoon I was expecting the police to call, to tell me that my wife had been savaged by the bitch—or worse, that Jenny was under arrest for cruelty to animals.

Nothing happened.

I arrived home to find the house peaceful. Lollo lay by the fire with her puppies. The boys were watching her feed them and making uninhibited remarks about the process.

Jenny looked smug.

"I've settled everything," she said.

She handed me the evening paper.

There, under Pets for Sale, was a notice.

FOR SALE—Eight dog puppies and seven bitch puppies. Unusual breed. £5 each, to good homes only.

"Jenny!" It was all I could find to say.

"I've sold all of them already," Jenny said smugly.

She began to laugh. "It's the first time any of your investments has shown a profit."

I looked at my wife, and she looked back at me, her eyes bright with amusement.

"Oh, Peter, you are a fool," she said, and rubbed her face against mine.

THE BOY AND THE DUKE'S BEAR

His name was Leopold; the same name as that of the Duke of Lorraine. It was the only thing he knew about himself. Both his parents had died of the plague that swept Savoy in that bitter cold winter of the 1870s, and he had been begging for food under the arches near the river.

He was a small boy, half-starved, so thin that his face was all bones and enormous eyes that stared forlornly up at the passers-by. They, well fed, and well dressed, felt guilty when they saw the child, and tossed him a coin. He could earn more money by holding the heads of the horses that drew the beautiful coaches and carriages.

They belonged to people who lived in a glorious world that he glimpsed through the open doorways of well furnished houses, with deep carpets and rich curtains; with servants in coloured liveries who opened and closed the doors. The women wore silks and satins, and had lovely faces; the children wore furs and the little girls hid their hands in muffs, and were plump and laughed a lot.

Leopold found little to laugh at. Sometimes he played with a stray kitten, or a forlorn dog, that was as hungry as he. He loved animals, and he shared his crumbs with most unlikely pets; with an old rat that had a hole under the lowest arch of the big bridge; with a field mouse that he had tamed and carried in his pocket; with the birds that waited as hungrily as he for the crumbs dropped by the rich.

There were so many boys like him, wandering alone, homeless. Some of them fought and robbed and stole, but Leopold never stole. His parents had been honest people, and until they died, he had a good home, even though it was very poor. There had always been soup and cheese and homemade bread to eat.

The nights were bitter, and he was desolate.

He huddled under the bridge, wondering if there were not somewhere warmer to lie at night.

He had been living rough for nearly eight months when old Anna found him. Anna was a country woman who had fallen on hard times herself, though not nearly so hard as these children. She had a little two-roomed home, and beside it she had a big barn, which could house a lot of bairns. She had once had a herd of cattle to care for; and a family. But now all were gone. She gathered a new family, of waifs and orphans, and these she fed twice daily with thick vegetable broth and good bread. They slept in the barn on the straw.

Leopold was no longer so hungry, although he still begged. His appealing eyes were a major asset and he could bring money to Anna for flour for the bread. There seemed to be more boys daily. They fought for the best places in the barn.

Leopold was one of the smallest of the boys. He had a draughty corner behind a manger, where the wind blew through, and even when he packed it hard with straw, there was a freezing breeze to chill his bones.

One night he left the barn and began to explore. There was a high wall, which he climbed, wondering if perhaps inside this boundary there was a rich man's estate, with outhouses. Perhaps there was a boilerhouse, where he would find warmth from the big ovens. If they were built into the wall, the bricks outside retained the heat and he could huddle there, out of the wind, against a chimney breast.

It was a very big estate. It belonged to Leopold, Duke of Lorraine. Little Leopold crept through the park, moonlight shining on the hoarfrost that trimmed the grass. There were big trees, and there was a summer house, but it was open to the wind, and cold.

Beyond it was a little hut. A closed hut, with a door that was held with a great latch that slipped into a hasp, and caught firm. There was a rustling inside the hut. A horse perhaps, and where there were horses there was warmth.

Leopold opened the door.

Inside was not a horse, but a great brown bear that stared at the boy from its tiny eyes. Leopold saw the thick fur coat. Warmth. His teeth were chattering, his bare feet were blue with cold, there were goose pimples all over him and he thought he would die of cold. Warmth emanated from the bear.

Warmth!

Leopold crept inside the hut, closing the door firmly behind him. He was not in the least afraid. It did not occur to him that an animal might harm him. He crawled into the straw, and settled down against the great beast's chest, and felt the heat of its body flow over him.

The bear, whose name was Marco, was a lonely beast. He put his great paws round the boy, and held him close, savouring companionship for the first time in his life. He had plenty of food, but little pleasure, coming out at long intervals to dance clumsily before the Duke, held firmly by a tight collar and a long chain that irked him.

Leopold slept warm and snug for the first time since his parents had died. He did not mind the smell of the great beast; nor did its teeth and jaws worry him. He burrowed into the fur, and the bear grunted with pleasure.

As soon as it was light, Leopold slipped out of the hut, shut the latch firmly, and ran through the bushes, to climb the wall, and return to the barn for his breakfast. He went back to the town to beg.

Very soon, he came nightly to the bear, climbing the wall as soon as it was dusk. Within a few days, Marco waited expectantly for the boy, needing nothing from him but his company, as Leopold never had food to spare. By the end of a month they were firm friends, and often the boy felt that the bear was the only creature in the whole world that loved him.

Marco too must have felt the same, for one night when Leopold arrived he found that there was still some food on the animal's plate; there were berries and apples; and some savouries from the Duke's table, for the Duke, when he remembered him, was fond of the big bear.

Leopold never had enough to eat, as Anna, with the best will in the world, had far too many mouths to feed, and because she couldn't bear to think of children starving, her menage grew almost daily. The boys ate and slept in the barn and by day flocked to the town to bring home what money they could. Leopold was never missed at night; his corner behind the manger was too uncomfortable for anyone else to take over, and no one bothered him once he had settled down. He only had to ease away the straw and slip through the hole, and he was away.

But there was one thing Leopold had not reckoned on. And that was snow. For he did not realise, leaving in the grey dawn, that on snowy mornings his footsteps were plain to see.

They were very small footprints, so the bearward knew that it was only a child that came at night. But the bear was not renowned for good temper, and the man, though rough and strict with the animal, making sure it was disciplined and did not harm anyone, was kind enough and he was intrigued.

One night, long after the bear had been shut in until morning, the man crept back and put his eye to a hole in the planks. What he saw amazed him, for the child was leaning comfortably against the bear, finishing off the tastiest titbits from a plate of food that the animal had been given well over three hours before.

Marco had an enormous appetite, and it was amazing that he should share his food like this. Once all the food was gone, the child licked the plate clean, holding it to his mouth, feeding like a little animal, and then he stretched himself and yawned and curled up in the straw, while Marco curled round him, one huge paw holding the boy close against him.

It was too good a story to keep to himself, but the Duke did not believe it. Marco had an unpredictable temper and more than once had smashed some beautiful object in rage, and also had taken a hatred to one of the courtiers, an effeminate man who wore a great deal of scent and who laughed at the animal and waved a handkerchief in his face. Marco had tried to kill the man, who had at least learned his lesson and never tried to torment the bear again.

"Come and see," the bearward said.

That night, the Duke and five of his court watched with the bearward. They were hidden among the trees, and saw the boy creep over the grass, and looking furtively to either side, slip into the hut. The Duke, who was a young man, raced across to peep, and watched the child take the food that the bear had saved for him, and then curl in the straw, hugged close against the bear's enormous chest.

They went away, and Leopold did not know that the other Leopold had watched him. He now knew the bear so well that they played together, although there was not much room in the little hut. They rolled together, the boy laughing, although he kept his voice low, afraid of being overheard.

The Duke and the courtiers went on watching, intrigued by the situation.

One night Leopold was too exhausted to eat. He left the food. He was cold; and then he was hot, his skin dry, and he coughed as he breathed. The Duke watched the bear try to make the child eat, pushing his head against the boy's legs; pushing the plate towards the child, obviously worried in his animal way at any creature refusing food.

Only then did the Duke realise this was no peepshow. The child was ill; and he had nowhere else to sleep. No one had given any real thought to the boy's situation.

He opened the door and the bearward held a torch so that the Duke could see. He dared not come near lest the flames fire the straw, but the light was enough to show the child's terrified face, as he clung to the bear, sure he would be executed for trespassing. He knelt in the straw, too frightened to speak.

"Come, child, we want to help you," the Duke said, and held out his ringed hand to the boy.

Leopold had never seen anyone with so many rings, or with such rich clothes. He was sure that the Duke was at least a king; and even more sure when he was led into the Duke's home, which was hung with tapestries, and in which there were many antiques. The child stared about him, but he was to ill and too bewildered to take much heed.

His life changed completely. He was bathed, to his horror, and put, in a capacious nightshirt, in a warm bed in a small attic, where one of the maids nursed him. He had nourishing soup and a place to sleep, and no longer any need to beg. He was cared for, and when he was better, he was dressed in rich clothes and became the Duke's pet. Often he crept back to Marco to talk to the bear, being ill at ease in the vast household, where he felt that he did not belong.

He loved talking to the bearward and helped look after the bear.

But winter returned and with winter came coughs and colds and Leopold caught a cold, and could not throw it off. He was once more confined to bed, but bed meant he could not see Marco and he loved the bear more than he loved any creature on earth and the bear loved him.

He crept out in the bitter cold, although he had been told not to go outside. He spent the night in the bear's hug; and they found him in the morning, too weak to return home.

They had been too late; his early years of running wild had weakened him beyond all hope of recovery, and Leopold died the next evening, trying to get out of his bed and return to the first creature that had shown him affection after he had been orphaned.

Marco became more and more surly; missing his companion, not wanting to dance, or to act for the court, and in the end, he too went.

But both of them by then had acquired fame, and the story was told again and again, of the boy who had slept, night after night, with the Duke's bad-tempered bear.

THE BIRTHDAY

Birthdays ought to be fun, Simon thought, battling viciously with wood and sticks and paper, trying to light the fire in the big old-fashioned grate in the cottage that had sounded such adventure.

His father had bought it two years ago and they had spent two summers there, in the deep country at the end of the lane, their nearest neighbour a farmhouse almost half a mile away.

It had been wonderful in summer, with the stream at the bottom of the overgrown garden; with the old walnut tree to climb, with blackberries to pick on autumn weekends when the wind sang high in the woods that backed on to their garden and the pheasants stalked regally and unafraid over the stubbled fields.

And then the blow had fallen. It wasn't really a tremendous blow, but it felt that way. Simon's father had to go to Australia for six months and he and his mother were on their own for the first time in their lives.

Almost alone. They had also had Hercules, their arrogant, evil, slant-eyed Siamese cat. Hercules who hated rain and who, when the heavens opened, stormed at the front door, and demanded that everyone should go with him to the back door to find out if it was raining there too.

Hercules could never understand why it should rain outside both doors and spent the wet days prowling from back to front, tail lashing, growly voice exclaiming nonstop and both Simon and his mother spent their time opening both doors one after the other to convince Hercules it was still raining out there.

'I'm sure he thinks we do it,' his mother had said, after one particularly bad day. Hercules was a very noisy companion.

The six months dragged, in spite of his father's long letters, with stories of a country outside Simon's imagining, where brilliantly plumaged parrots flew in noisy flocks across the land, and koala bears cried in the blue gum trees, and wallabies and kangaroos were familiar sights when you went out into the country.

'It's so big,' his father wrote. 'You can never imagine how big, or how desolate the forests are, with dead trees that have been there since the beginning of time, and high banked rivers, and the sun shining.'

Simon lit a match which spurted into a small flame and then went out. His birthday was just before Christmas, on the shortest day of the year, and his mother had decided, as they were going to be quite alone and had no relations at all, that they would go to the cottage for the Christmas holidays, just she and Simon and the cat.

'Think what fun it will be,' she said, and Simon had visions of the cottage, warm and cosy with a bright fire burning, and the curtains drawn to shut out the dark, and the long evenings, just the three of them, and days spent in gathering firewood in the wood, and his birthday spent in excitement.

It was nothing like that at all.

Outside a lowering sky delivered snow and more snow. Snow that piled clammily against the back door and on the window sills. Snow that clung to the window sills and melted and made pools inside the frame; snow that came down the bedroom chimney; that slithered off the roof in the night so that Hercules swore loudly and refused to be comforted, and prowled noisily, telling off imaginary burglars until both Simon and his mother were sure there was someone outside.

And in the morning it was very plain that Simon's mother had flu. Her face was flushed, her head ached, her legs ached, and her nose ran.

'I'm sorry, love,' she said forlornly through a fog of misery. 'I'll just have to stay in bed. We'll celebrate your birthday tomorrow and pretend today hasn't happened.'

HAPPY BIRTHDAY SIMON, said the card on the

table. His mother must have painted it last night, after he had gone up to bed.

The room was icy.

He had longed, in their centrally heated flat, for a real coal fire. But the reality was ashes in the morning and a fine feathery dust that flew all over the rug when he tried to rake them out. The reality was damp wood and paper that blazed and died before the wood caught, and a burn at the top of his finger from an incautiously lighted match.

He had got up early, and made his mother a cup of tea. He had let Hercules out, though Hercules had complained that he didn't like the snow, that he didn't need to go out, that he would much rather stay in, he was cold and it was time that fire was alight, so that he could curl up and watch the flames. So that he could roll on his back and turn his tummy to the blaze and bask blissfully, eyes half-closed, slender black paws kneading the hearth-rug.

Simon looked at the reluctant fire. There was a faint hint of light on the wood, a tiny glimmer that he might be able to fan into a blaze.

He bent down and blew.

A fine way to spend a birthday.

At last the fire lit. It was a sulky smouldering smoky fire, but at least it was alight. He added more wood, and put the guard securely in place, and then went to call Hercules.

He had been so busy he had not noticed that it was snowing again.

He stared at the garden, which had vanished under an even whiteness. It was snowing so hard that there was not even a pawmark to show where Hercules had gone. And there was no sign of the cat. Worse, there was no sound of the cat.

Simon shivered, looking over the top of the snow, seeing how deep it lay, and how it masked the trees and the gate and the hedge. It was bitterly cold.

He had known snow in the town where he lived; a few inches on the pavements, swiftly swept away; turning to dark slush, lying briefly and melting fast. He had never imagined anything like this. The fields had gone. The hedges had vanished. The trees were laden, their branches bowed to the ground. If he had realised how deep it was he would never have let the cat go out.

He stepped on to the path, forgetting the doorstep was high. He plunged, knee deep, and fell, floundering in the snow. He stopped and brushed himself off and stared, frightened now, at the unbroken surface.

He called the cat, very softly.

There was not a sound, not even a bird noise. The whole world had vanished behind the swirling flakes.

He dared not tell his mother how deep the snow was, or that Hercules was out in it. They had had Hercules for five years and the cat was their most precious possession. Simon thought of him now, out there in the bitter cold. The snow might lie for days; and the cat would die.

He swallowed a lump in his throat and made toast and spread butter and marmalade and made more tea. His mother could not eat. He stared at her, worried, and she managed to smile.

'I'll be better in the morning,' she said. 'I only hope you don't catch it too, Simon. It's not much of a way to spend a birthday.'

'It doesn't matter,' Simon said. He took the tray downstairs and made himself some toast but he couldn't eat it. He stared out of the window at the falling flakes. It was past time for the milkman, but he did not come. Luckily there were tins of milk in the pantry. The newspaper did not come either, nor the post. That was the most disappointing of all, for even if he did save his birthday till his mother was better there might have been a parcel from his father, an exciting shape to look at, and feel, and guess at, and to know his father had not forgotten him. Their neighbours in the next flat had promised to redirect their mail.

Hercules had never seen snow in his life. He was not allowed out in the town, where he might get killed by a car. His world was bounded by the walls of the flat and he had an earth box in the bathroom, and no freedom at all. He spent much of his time on the windowsill grumbling at the pigeons who dared to alight on the sill.

Their flat was part of an old house, which had been marooned among the housing estates. The garden had gone, as the house had been extended, and there were ten families living there now. No one minded cats. Most of the families had a cat or kept gerbils or hamsters and one family had a dog. A poodle, Marco, that had been taught to bark without making a noise.

His soundless bark was a party trick.

Hercules loved the cottage; he spent his time in the garden, pouncing on imaginary mice. He found exciting smells and enticing holes down which he could put his paw. He found a jungle where he could hide and a place where he could bask in the hot sun.

Winter was less exciting. It was cold and damp and his sorties into the garden were brief.

Snow was different.

The sun had been shining when Simon let him out and the cat trod on the crisp surface, patted at the white flakes that fell from a bush and negotiated the path delicately, intrigued by the strange sensation of falling through the ground at every step. He patted an overhanging branch and was showered in soft flakes.

He walked down the path to the gate. There was a sparrow feeding on berries on the other side of the lane. The snow was so deep that Hercules sank at every step, but it was not deep enough to alarm him. His eyes on the sparrow, he leaped.

He fell.

He fell through soft snow into a deep hole filled with water.

He cried aloud but Simon was upstairs with his mother's tea and did not hear.

The snow closed over Hercules' head.

The slow minutes passed.

Nobody came.

By lunchtime Simon was frightened.

His mother was worse and there was no sign anywhere of the cat. It had stopped snowing, but the country had lost its landmarks. Everywhere looked alike, and he was not even sure that he could find his way to the farm.

He would have to try. His mother needed a doctor. Suppose she had to go to the hospital, or had pneumonia? Suppose he ended up here all alone over Christmas, and suppose Hercules never came back?

There had never been a birthday like this, not for anyone, ever, Simon thought desperately.

He went back upstairs. His mother had been asleep, but she woke as he came into the room.

'I'm going to the farm to phone for the doctor,' he said.

'Darling, I'm so sorry. But I do feel so ill.'

'Will you be all right while I'm gone?' Simon hoped she would not get out of bed and look out of the window and see the deep snow.

She only nodded and closed her eyes. She was like him, small and dark and blue-eyed, but her eyes were brilliant now with dark shadows round them and the colour in her normally pale cheeks was high.

Simon dressed warmly, putting on an extra jersey under his fleece-lined and hooded anorak. He put on a second pair of trousers, and thick socks in his boots.

He opened the door and went outside.

The cold tore at his throat. He gasped, and was glad of the sheepskin gloves his father had given him the year before. They had been too big at first but now they were snugly fitting.

It had stopped snowing.

The sky had cleared to a brilliant blue and the ground glittered. Simon looked for pawmarks but there were none and the fear for Hercules was as great as the fear for his mother.

He sank into the snow at every step.

He had learned from his fall to keep feeling his way and had picked up his father's walking stick, in order to prod the ground. It wouldn't do to fall into a drift or the ditch. Perhaps Hercules was in the ditch. . . .

Simon turned to the right when he reached the gate. He floundered along the lane, using the stick to push against the hedge, to make sure that he did not wander into the fields, and get lost. He had never been so frightened in his life. The world had vanished and he was all alone.

Behind him, deep holes marked his footprints.

At last he saw a feather of smoke in the air. He could aim directly for the farm now, and he tried to hurry, but only succeeded in falling headlong, so that once more he slowed down, taking care. He was so worried that it was hard not to sob but he was far too old for tears. He was the man of the house with his father away, and everything depended on him.

He turned the corner between high walls of snow that had drifted against the hedge. The farmer and the shepherd were there with two dogs. Behind them, in the farmyard, sheep bleated noisily.

'Simon.' The farmer stared at him. 'What on earth are you doing here?'

'My mother's ill. She needs a doctor. She's very ill,' Simon said. 'And we've lost Hercules.'

Everyone knew Hercules. The handsome brown and black seal point greeted all passers-by noisily and favoured a few, including the farmer, with a rub around the ankles and a deep throaty purr.

'Shepherd was coming down with the snow plough and your milk.' the farmer said. 'And postman's been with two parcels for you. I thought you'd manage till lunchtime, knowing your Ma had a good stock of food. Afraid the line's down, lad. Shepherd had better take the plough into the village and get the doctor up. I'll come back with you and bring the dog and we'll see if we can find your cat, and Mother'll come along and see to your Ma. If you got here, she can get there.'

The journey back to the cottage was less frightening, with the farmer and his plump cheerful wife to distract him from his worries.

'There's a lot of flu about,' the farmer's wife said. 'It's nasty for a day or two, but it only lasts a short while. If Shepherd clears the road between us I can get to and fro easy enough and help out. You did well to get through to us, lad. It's nasty round here when it snows.'

Simon took the farmer's wife indoors. She poked the fire to a blaze and added more wood, and within seconds had the kettle on and was making a cup of beef tea, having brought a jar with her.

'Nothing like it,' she said. 'You go and help Dad look for your cat. He's got Nan with him and Nan can find a buried sheep as quick as kiss your hand; no need to worry about Hercules. He can't be far and cats have nine lives.'

Simon went outside, relieved to know his mother was in such capable hands. The farmer was standing at the gate, watching his collie bitch. She was tiny, with a sleek black body and white paws and a white tip on her tail, and fringed wide-set eyes that looked back constantly for praise and reassurance.

'Seek, girl. Good girl, seek,' the farmer said.

Nan plunged deep at every step, but her eager nose sniffed and her busy tail wagged continuously. She loved working; and she knew she was looking for something alive, though she did not know what.

She zigzagged across the lane and back, across and back, until her tracks overlapped everywhere in the snow.

She came to the edge of the lane.

She paused by the side of it and suddenly she began to dig, with snow flying out behind her. The farmer ran and began to dig with his hands and Simon joined them, frantically enlarging the hole that Nan had made.

Nan stopped digging and backed off, barking shrilly.

'Dear heaven, the cat's in a hole in the ground,' the farmer said, peering down. Hercules had fallen through the snow into a hole dug in the lane at the edge of the ditch. Simon suddenly remembered the roadmen had been there the day before the snow began. He had forgotten all about the hole. A good job he hadn't fallen into it too. The farmer had knocked snow from a wooden barrier that had guarded the beginning of a new trench to lay a sewer to the cottage. They did not have mains drainage. Only a cesspit in the field behind the garden and the council had declared it needed replacing.

Simon floundered down the garden to the shed. Snow

lay against the door and he kicked it away and pushed with his shoulders, clearing a space. Time had ceased, was dragging on limping feet, time was vital. The cat was in water at freezing point, or only just above as there was no ice yet; when he got too cold he would give up struggling and drown.

The shed door needed a key.

The key was hanging on a nail inside the kitchen door. Simon blundered back into the cottage, grabbed the key and forced his way back to the shed. Snow seemed such fun when you thought of it for skiing and tobogganing and for making snowmen. It wasn't nearly such fun when you needed the doctor and animals were buried and time was essential and you had to break a path at every step.

The key was rusty and wouldn't turn.

Simon was so frustrated that he yelled with anger. The farmer ran towards him, floundering clumsily and hurled himself against the shed door, splintering it around the lock. He grabbed the spade and went back to the lane where Nan was digging again.

It was beginning to freeze. The sky had darkened again, and it was bitterly cold, colder than it had been when Simon left home. Simon fell and gasped with pain, almost sobbing as the breath was driven from his body.

The farmer attacked the snow viciously, sending it flying, digging busily, until the ground around the hole was exposed. The cat had been clinging to the earthy sides, but even while he dug, there was a small anguished yowl, and Hercules dropped out of sight with an immense splash, falling completely under the water.

The farmer stepped on to the cleared earth and dropped flat, but he could not see the cat. He jumped into the hole, after probing with Simon's stick to make sure that it was not too deep. The water was knee deep and bitter cold. He reached down, feeling under the icy surface until he could feel the cat's body. He dragged him up. For those last few moments Hercules had been completely submerged.

Simon stared at the bedraggled cat. Hercules looked dead. His eyes were closed and his body was limp. The farmer was shivering, his feet icy, his toes already numb, a wicked wind cutting through the wet trousers freezing on his chilled legs. He tucked the cat inside his coat and hurried to the cottage.

Simon followed; was the cat alive?

He couldn't be dead, not on Simon's birthday. Nothing could be as bad as that.

The farmer's wife was waiting for them.

'Your Ma's asleep,' she said. 'I've given her two asprins, and made her bed and she's two nice hot water bottles and the fire on up there.'

She looked at her husband.

'You get upstairs and in a hot bath. I'm sure Mrs Grant won't mind. There's plenty of hot water. It's a gas geyser. And give me that cat.'

There was a whimper at the door, and Simon went back to let Nan in. The bitch shook herself and snow flew all over the hall floor.

'You get down there, and be quiet,' the farmer's wife said.

'And you go and get towels, as many as you can find, out of the airing cupboard, Simon,' she said, and Simon kicked off his boots and ran, glad to be useful.

When he came back the farmer's wife had the cat on her lap, rubbing away at its body. She wrapped Hercules in the big towel that Simon brought.

'Is there another hot water bottle?' she asked.

Simon nodded. His mother had expected the beds to be damp, as the cottage had been empty for so long, and had brought six bottles with her. They had three each at night, and needed them, as the upstairs rooms were so cold.

'Fill any you can find, boy,' the farmer's wife said.

Simon went out, and when he had gone the farmer's wife unwrapped the cat and looked at him. His head hung lifeless and he did not seem to be breathing at all. His paws did not even twitch.

The farmer's wife rubbed, but nothing happened.

She had been born on a farm and lived on a farm and she had reared lambs and calves and pups and kittens and she wasn't going to be beaten now. She opened the cat's mouth and bent her head and began to breathe into the cat's mouth.

In. Out.

In. Out.

In. Out.

Simon came back into the room and stared at the farmer's wife, appalled. He carried two hot water bottles, and came to stand beside her, and watch, holding his own breath, a knot building inside him.

In. Out.

In. Out.

He put down the hot water bottles, knowing the cat was dead. He went to look out of the window, to look at the snow, hating it. Death-bringing snow. Bitter cold snow. Snow, cutting them off from the rest of the world.

He was conscious of the farmer's wife's deep slow breaths.

In. Out.

In. Out.

There was a sudden gasp.

Simon turned. Hercules flickered his eyes. He gasped again, a deep shuddering breath, and the farmer's wife turned him over as water spilled from his lungs. His legs twitched.

She began to rub, hard and vigorously.

'Put more wood on the fire, Simon,' she said, and her busy hands rubbed away the water, rubbed the draggled fur, rubbed warmth into the shivering body.

The farmer came downstairs looking unfamiliar in Simon's father's dressing gown. He stoked the fire expertly.

The farmer's wife discarded the soaking towel and took another and began to rub again, talking gently to the cat, soothing, soft voiced, murmuring. The logs crackled and spat, and flames flickered in the chimney, danced on the metal bowl on the table, glowed in miniature in Hercules' open eyes.

'Any brandy, lad?' the farmer asked. 'Me and the cat could both do with a bit of medicine.'

There was brandy in the sideboard. The farmer poured a few drops into a saucer of warm milk. The farmer's wife put Hercules down on the rug and he lapped greedily.

'He's as strong as a horse,' the farmer said, pouring himself a small dose of brandy. 'He'll get over that lot in no time.'

The collie bitch had left her corner and come to the hearth-rug to sniff at the cat. Her mothering instincts roused, she began to lick him. Hercules knew Nan well. She visited in the summer. He curled, savouring the blaze, and the bitch curled round his still damp body. The farmer's wife padded one of the hot water bottles and slipped it under the cat.

'He'll be all right now,' she said.

Simon nodded, unable to speak. He hoped he would never live through anything quite as bad as the last few hours. Hercules began to purr.

The doorbell rang.

'That's Shepherd with the doctor, I'll be bound,' the farmer said.

Simon went to the door.

Shepherd was at the gate, sitting on the cab of the snow plough, and two men stood on the doorstep. Simon stared, and a moment later was crushed in a bear hug.

'Dad,' he yelled.

'Didn't you get my letter?' his father asked, filling the hall, shaking snow, directing the doctor upstairs and walking into the sitting room all in one breath.

It was some time before Simon managed to tell him all the story. Later that day, when the farmer and his wife had gone and Shepherd had brought back some medicine for his mother, Simon and his father sat on her bed, and cut Simon's cake. Simon opened his parcels; a book from his mother and a pair of knitted gloves from the farmer's wife; and with the post was a telegram that he hadn't yet seen.

'COMING HOME EARLY,' it read. And was signed Dad.

'I finished the job earlier than I expected,' his father

said. 'I wasn't sure if I could make it for your birthday. In all the flap I've lost my luggage and your present's inside.'

'I don't mind,' Simon said, meaning every word. His mother was better, his father was home and Hercules was sitting beside his mother, curled up close against her, with a hot water bottle beneath him.

His deep throbbing purr filled the room.

Simon looked at him; at his smoky back and his black tail and paws; at his black mask and black ears and the almond-shaped blue eyes with their deep black pupils, that stared at him as if Hercules was trying to talk.

The room was warm. Flames flickered in the hearth, and his father had made a super birthday tea, and outside shadows lay on the snow.

'Tomorrow we'll go tobogganing,' his father said, and stretched himself and yawned.

'And Hercules will stay in until the snow clears.'

'Waugh' said Hercules, agreeing with every word.

Simon laughed.

He had thought at the beginning of the day that it had been the worst birthday he had ever had in his life.

Now he thought it was the best.

It was funny how things turned out, he thought that night as he lay in bed.

Snow slithered off the roof.

A paw patted at his face.

Hercules was cold and Simon was warm. Hercules wasn't allowed in beds. But just for once. . . .

Simon lifted the sheet and Hercules crept inside.

When his father came to say goodnight Simon was asleep and a small hump in the bed was purring loudly.

Simon's father smiled to himself as he shut the door.

STAR OF THE DESERT

The silver mare was the most beautiful mare in the whole of Araby. The bearded Sheikh was the wisest man in the whole of Araby. Soon the mare would have a foal.

Outside in the dark the wind whispered and teased the sand. The sand rustled under stars that shone bright and clear and cold and faraway. Inside the silken tent the Sheikh waited, and the mare waited for her son, and her brown eyes were dark with longing for the foal that would soon be born.

Beyond the silken curtains the Sheikh's children waited and whispered too. Was the foal born yet? Would he be strong? Would he be faster than the white winged birds that flew across the shimmering sky? Would his coat gleam with a shine of light? The mare's coat gleamed and when she fled across the sand she was silver splendour, swifter than sunlight and racing shadows, faster then windrush, and fleeter than the speeding birds.

To the Sheikh, she was all delight and he prized her more than the jewels in his coffers, more than all the gold in the taxes he raised from his people, almost more than his life.

Her name was Windsong, and when he rode her he left the sad daily world far behind and knew only the joy of racing through the singing gales. The sound of her hooves sighing in the sand, the feel of her power beneath him as he rode to glory.

The children whispered. The stars shone bright. The wind rustled the sand and the Sheikh waited, and the mare waited and dreamed, knowing that soon a new life would lie beside her; a new foal to grow into a fine son, for this was her fourth foal, and she loved her younglings with a love that was as great as any human mother's for her baby child.

'Soon, my beauty, soon,' the wise Sheikh said softly, and his brown hands soothed her silver coat and he spoke quietly. He praised her for her gentleness and her soft velvet lips that nuzzled his chest and the silken sleekness of her coat. He praised the deep darkness of her longlashed eyes. He fed her with warm camel milk, that he had taken himself from Starshine, the queen of his camels.

The mare drank deep. She drank from a bucket of silver, patterned with tiny foals that galloped endlessly round the rim. Beyond her was the soft white and scarlet saddle, and her jewelled harness, and the bright ruby that shone from the centre of her headbands.

'Queen of queens,' the wise Sheikh said, 'give me a fine foal to cherish among my horses. Give me a star beyond rubies, give me a foal with long legs for running and a deep chest and sound heart. Give me a foal that will be the most beautiful foal in all of Araby. For you are my priceless treasure, my pride, and all my joy.'

Beyond the silken curtains the children whispered and waited and excitement ran high. Was the foal born yet? They dared not ask, for the wise Sheikh could be very angry with a forward child. The jewelled and bright-clad women waited too, soothing the children and feeding them, for the mare needed peace.

'Hush, little ones,' the women said.

The wind was growing to an angry blast that whirled the sand and hid the stars. The night was darkened and the silken tents were hidden in a swirl of sand. The children shivered, afraid, and their mothers lifted and held them, and sang to drown the terror of the noisy dark.

Peace, my little one, peace,
Cease to fret,
Sleep, my little one, sleep.
Sleep, my pet.

The women sang softly and their voices drowned the angry wind, and soothed the waiting mare, and the Sheikh massaged her coat, and his fingers comforted her, for the waiting was long.

Beyond the silken curtain the children slept. Their mothers laid them on their beds, and covered them with embroidered shawls, and smiled among themselves, and sat and listened to the wind winging wildly through the starry dark, and the deep voice of the wisest Sheikh in all of Araby as he spoke words of comfort to his mare.

Dawn came and the wind noise fell to a whisper and the only star in the sky was the morning star. The women and children slept and the day was still. Only the wise Sheikh watched, his bearded face weary with waiting all the night.

The mare stood and arched her neck and lifted her tail and her foal fell and the Sheikh caught it in his hands. It was alive and breathing. Kicking long legs, struggling to free itself from the birth cover that masked its head.

The Sheikh cut the cover and the mare stood to her son; the waiting hours forgotten. Together they dried his soft damp coat. The wise Sheikh knelt in the straw and rubbed the delicate legs that would, one day, be strong, and the mare caressed her son, her dark eyes deep mirrors of shining pride.

'See how clever I am,' her eyes seemed to say to the Sheikh. 'See my beautiful foal.'

When the sun was high the foal stood up to feed. He was as graceful as a young gazelle, his tiny body promising strength, his deep chest promising that he would run far and fast and fleet, and his lovely head lifted to his mother for the kiss that told him that he was hers and she was his, and he was her much-loved son.

The children waited and whispered and could not be still, for they knew the foal was born. At last the foal was fed, and the mother soothed and fed too, and bedded on fresh straw.

'Come, but come quietly,' the wise Sheikh said, and the children came, their brown faces alive with excitement, their dark eyes lost in wonder.

'Aaah' the children said. 'He is so beautiful.'

'He is the most beautiful foal in all the world,' the wise Sheikh said. 'And he who tends him, and gentles him, and rides upon his back attains high honour. There is nothing so noble as a horse, and this, the little one, my Star of the Desert, is more noble than any yet born. Now, let him sleep.'

The children went through the silken curtain. They had no words, for the mare and the little foal were lovelier than dreams. Outside in the desert the wind soothed the hot midday sand, and the sun shone from a clear blue sky and men sought the shade and spoke of the new foal.

Inside the silken tent the mare nosed her son, and the wise Sheikh slept at last, lying on his silken bed beside them, never leaving them, day or night. He woke and prayed to his God, thanking him for the splendid foal.

Star of the Desert lay close beside his mother, and did not know that he was the most beautiful foal in the whole of Araby, or that he belonged to the wisest Sheikh in the whole of Araby.

The children knew. They whispered beyond the silken curtain and excitement ran high as they spoke of the wonderful future that awaited their father's foal, and they dreamed his dream for him. Star of the Desert. There was indeed no foal like him in the whole of Araby.

KILLERS ON THE TRAIL

The killers were on the prowl. Twenty feet of solid power, black bodies slashed with white, cruising in search of food as the great grampuses, the deadly killer whales, cut through the green water.

The sea leopard waited on the edge of the ice floe. His ten foot long mottled body was still, a dark blur against the bruised yellow snow. Beyond him, just in sight over the ice ledge, an Adelie penguin brooded her egg, the precious object resting on her feet, guarded by the hot flap of skin that formed a brood pouch, and helped incubate the chick.

She was unaware of the watcher. Her mate was fishing and she waited patiently for her own turn. The male penguin surfaced. She shuffled towards him, eager to be relieved of her burden.

The sea leopard crouched, ready to spring. His body arched. The killers surfaced. They saw him, and charged the floe.

The impact caught him off balance and he skidded along the ice into the sea. The penguins, only now aware of danger, yet unable to run because of the precious egg, huddled together in terror.

The sea leopard forgot them. His seal-like body shot through the water, ten feet of thrusting speed, pursued by giant death.

The packed killers fanned out. Two on either flank, the fifth behind. The sea leopard accelerated. Teeth raked his absurdly tiny tail, giving him impetus.

He dived. The sudden change of direction caught the killers by surprise. They overshot their quarry and turned in a flurry of water that marked the surging waves with flecks of foam.

The sea leopard, impelled by fear, hurled himself beneath a broken floe, and clambered on to the far side, trying to regain his breath. He realised, as soon as he reached solid ground, that his haven was far too small. The charging whales could smash his sanctuary in a few seconds.

As the five high fins broke the smooth swell, he dived long and deep, skimming towards the solid edge of pack ice fringing the island. Here was safety; here he could hurry with his ungainly flap and shuffle, and leave the sea behind, escaping from the wide terrifying jaws.

He came up for air, and was dazzled by the sun flashing on black backs and white underparts. He moaned in terror as his incautious head hit the underside of one of the whales.

The killer arched and span. Its mouth gaped towards him. The sea leopard somersaulted in the water, and left his heavier pursuers hunting in futile bewilderment as he sped away.

Five fins still pointed to the sky.

The sea leopard knew he could never reach safety. The land was too far away. And he was tiring.

He breathed deeply and submerged. Below the island, twisted rocks hid caves, and deep reefs thrust out into the sea. Fish, swimming peacefully in sub-aquatic tunnels, panicked and fled as the sea leopard dropped among them.

There was little room to spare.

He flicked his tail and turned, facing the entrance. Two pairs of eyes stared balefully at him, white markings blurring the dark outlines.

He settled to wait. Too long under water, and it might be too late ever to breathe again, but his stored air would hold for some time yet.

Angry bodies butted against rock. The sea leopard watched, hidden in the darkness.

The water throbbed.

Beyond the lurking shapes was the glistening balloon-like body of a white whale. The killers heard it. They turned and packed again, giving chase to a more convenient prey.

When the water stilled the sea leopard swam out. He cruised towards the surface.

Seconds later he crouched on the ice, devouring a large cod that had swum unwarily towards him.

So little time had passed that beyond him, on another floe, the two penguins completed their task of transferring their egg from one pair of feet to another. The male settled comfortably, and brooded it, thoughtfully.

The female dived for fish and fed until she was bursting.

The sea leopard slept, as the killer pack continued their long hunting.

THE RAG TAG CHASE

You want to know how I got these scratches? You'll never believe me if I tell you. It was all because of hunting. Not the kind of hunting you'd think of now.

The nobs can keep their handsome hunters, their well-bred hounds, and their pink coats. I'll wager my flea-bitten gelding to a piece of Ballymeeny bog that they never had a day's hunting like ours, just two weeks ago come next Friday.

There was Paddy Joe Rafferty on his great grey nag, the Tinker's Curse, a rangy old horse, with a ride like a boat in a westerly gale, and legs like pistons, flailing along. There was Morris Sweeny, the blacksmith, on Nightmare, a great black creature that the police once looked at and never bought. She'd every vice that any horse ever thought of, and a few they haven't, besides.

There was Willy Bye from the farm at Suicide's Cross, if ye can call a few acres of bog, and a pig, and a goat, and a cow, a farm. He was riding Father Flynn's Folly, a horse that near broke the good father's neck and that he sold to Willy for free eggs for the rest of his life. Father Flynn's life, that is, and I haven't made out yet who has the worst of that bargain. Willy Bye's chickens lay in the heather, and cunning they are at hiding the eggs.

I was riding my flea-bitten gelding, as big as the Tinker's Curse and broader. He was bred for racing, out of as fine a mare as ever won the Oaks in England, and win it she did, way back, before you were ever dreamed of. But her lad wasn't watching and she mismatched herself with a Shire stallion that leaped six hedges to get at her. The foal she almost died of bearing is as big as a Shire with the speed of a racehorse, and the only thing to do when he gets the bit between his teeth is to hang on to his mane, and curse, and pray, and yell to the kids to scatter. His name's Hurricane and it's a name to suit him.

So there we are. I'm Danny O'Flynn, and me da is the baker and I do any job going, from working on the roads to helping at the harvest. I was never a man to settle, and I like my poteen, and ye cannot work the next day after a night with the lads. So I take my work as I find it and it's a better life than most men have, I'm telling ye that.

Those are the horses we were riding. And now for our dogs. There's Rusty, Paddy Joe's whippet, with a turn of speed on him that I've never seen bettered. That is, when he's a mind, which isn't often. And Morris's lurcher that's a good dog with the rabbits. Bowls them clean over, and stuns them, or so Morris says. All he has to do is pick them up, and feeling sorry for the poor brutes, he puts them swiftly out of their misery.

He never confesses the rabbits, but the hares trouble his conscience and Father Flynn gives him absolution and takes the hare from him. His housekeeper is a good cook and her jugged hare a dish to remember for ever, I'm told.

There's Willie's wee Jack Russell, Trot, that has killed three vixens and fifteen weasels and is as mean a creature as any Jack Russell ever bred, and that's saying something. It's an odd breed and I know more rogues than most among it.

And there's my pup, Pewter, that's steely coloured and bred from a mis-match of a labrador and a chow, and the result of that mated herself to a springer spaniel. Morris says I've a new breed with its labrador body and steely coat and the long black spaniel ears. A chowlabaniel. Enough to make an undertaker laugh. But Pewter can hunt and has a nose on him any police dog would envy.

It was Fred who started us. He's an Englishman, but he's a great fellow for all that, and nobody's his equal at fishing or shooting. He lets his rooms to the fishermen and deer hunters. Many a laugh we have at the Martyr's Retreat, over the men who fish all day; and the trout swim backwards in shoals and jeer at them; and the men who can't hit a deer if they put the rifle to its eye; or who blaze away at an old tree branch, convinced it's a stag's antlers.

Fred rents some thousands of acres, with three lakes and a tidy bit of river. He raises store cattle, and breeds springers (which is how I got Pewter. Off his dog, by mistake, as I thought my bitch had finished her season. Four days over three weeks she was, and then had nine puppies). And he has chickens and he said he had foxes. Dozens of foxes. So we said we'd see what we could do.

We met on a dream of a day with the sun shining and the grass drenched in dew, to run a fox from Robin's Acre, where Fred said the big rogue lay. The horses were eager and the dogs were wild to hunt, and the going was rough, over bracken and bramble, through mire and mud, with no chance of the fox out of cover the whole of the way. Fred promised to drink us under the table at his own expense if we killed. The rogue had too many of Fred's ducks and chickens packed into his belly.

Pewter found, and yelled, and we saw the red flash as the old beast came out of cover, saw the streak of fur that was his back and him going well and the dogs behind him, and ye should have heard the thunder of hooves and the crackle of dead wood as the horses shattered the branches.

He was through the hedge at the end of the lane and the three dogs after him. Up went the Folly and thumped down hard and was away, and Hurricane went over, no style at all, and I near broke me nose on his head, as he flung it back as he landed, and me in mid air and no stirrups at all and grabbing his mane. We're not the classiest riders, as you'll have gathered.

The Tinker's Curse broke a hole in the hedge big enough for Patrick Mahon's old bus, and the Nightmare thought up a new trick and stopped dead. Morris went over her head and sat on the hedge, just his nose showing and sure enough he'd need to go to confession for the things he said. The Nightmare had shown her feelings and now showed willing. She climbed that hedge, hauling herself over like a darn great cat, and landed the other side in a mudhole, and Morris thought of some new ways to describe her as he dragged her out.

He got aboard and on we thundered and the birds

screamed as we came. Jay and magpie, crow and starling, and all the little ones too, till ye'd think the devil himself was hunting, so great a noise they made.

Down the overgrown path between the trees, with the whippy branches lashing back in our faces, and Morris Sweeny's old cloth cap knocked off his head hitting the Hurricane fair and square on the muzzle, terrifying him so that he turned out a hell of a speed I never knew he had, accelerating like Micky O'Shea the postman the day he had a young hare in his bag with the letters and met the police sergeant on the way home.

We pelted through the bracken, flew across the hedge and ditch, and far behind us I heard the Tinker's Curse panting, the wind in his lungs whistling worse than usual. Paddy Joe bought him for a few pounds and a jar or so of poteen and no questions asked, but the poor brute has always been broken-winded. A crime to ride him, Father Flynn says, but he's never felt the same about horses since the Folly threw him the length of County Clare and ye know what the soil is like there. All rock. No wonder the man sold the horse. I'd have done the same meself.

By now we were all well away and there was a flash of tawny showing and Misty was running like the flying autumn wind, and Trot was gamely loping behind, small as maybe, just a streak of white showing now and then in the bracken. After them, stopping to scratch the ants off him, came Pewter. He'd ears almost green with the burrs sticking to him, poor brute.

At the end of the field is a stream, cutting through the peat, the ground wet and boggy, and the horses labouring and the dogs going badly but the old fellow himself away, just a ginger flash in the distance; not even a proper glimpse of him. Pewter gave tongue and Trot gave ground and Rusty gave up and paddled in the stream and out again, and came and shook himself, and the bright drops flew in the sun and wetted the Tinker's Curse who hates water anyway.

The old horse gathered himself to jump the stream and clear the water but he misjudged. He came down with a splash that soaked all three of us, and soaked his rider, who cursed and drove him up the bank and on, and yelled at the lurcher, but Rusty had lost interest. He was away on a trail of his own and that was the last anyone saw of him for three days, when he came home tired and muddy and slept for twenty-four hours and never moved a whisker.

We pounded on, our horses plastered with mud and the peat bog wet beneath us, and the bright lake to the south of us, and the birds singing in the shivering rushes until they heard our coming and then there was no sound at all from them. We pulled up our horses for a breather by the derelict boathouse and heard the little waves splashing and the wind sighing in the rustling leaves, and the panting of our horses and not another sound.

High above us a kestrel hovered, watching. Maybe he thought he could jump the old fox too, but it would be more than a mouthful for the bird, and he was mistaken. He was no doubt watching the wave in the grass where the rascal ran, thinking it was a rat maybe, or something smaller for him to grab.

We raced on, but slower now and all of us tiring, past the big house, thundering over the gravel, down by the other side of the lake, and past the landing stage where the fishermen stared at us. A black labrador barked at Trot, and he stopped to fight, and that was the last that we saw of him. Behind us came a snarling and a snapping, and yelling, and a shouting to us to come and call our dog off, but we had no time. Only Pewter was left to run the old beast and there was still a ginger flash in the bushes.

We swept on, stampeding along the path beside the river, where the rushes grew thicker still and offered cover, and we wondered if the beast would take to the water and swim and then we would lose it for sure as horses and dog were winded. I'd lost me whip and could feel the horse sweating and somewhere far behind us Willy had dropped out too. We could hear him cursing, but on we sped, and on, along the river and into a field, and into another field and over a hedge, and over a ditch, and into the bog, and out again and by now the children were shouting us on as they came out of school.

Down the boreen we went, past the schoolhouse, the children screeching with excitement, the ginger flash speeding through the gardens, and not along the road at all. We came to the farmyard behind my cottage, and there the old beast flew over the wall, turned plumb crazy, and leaped towards me with a hellish screech and on to my horse, and clawed at my face.

Morris Sweeny caught up and laughed till the tears came down his cheeks, a yell of laughter that the children echoed as I fought off my own old ginger tomcat that had led us as merry a dance as any fox led any hunt in the whole of Ireland.

That's how I got my scratches and he's not forgiven me yet, old Ginger, but runs whenever he sees me or the horse or the dog, and I don't blame him. I'd surely run meself if I were him and saw me coming.

For all that he led us a pretty chase, and I'm not grudging him the end of it, poor old brute. But me mam isn't speaking to me, and Morris Sweeny looks sheepish when he sees me, and Willy Bye looks at me, and laughs, and the whole village talks of the rag tag chase and the day that Danny O'Flynn went hunting and never caught a fox at all, but was caught by his own tomcat.

THE INNOCENT

It was very quiet in the church. Even the sound of gunfire was muted. It had been snowing and the snow blanketed noise. Blue shadows were cast upwards on blinded windows, where wood covered the shattered panes. The light of late evening shone through the arch above the altar, filling the gloom with gold. The child stood in the aisle and looked towards the altar. He had never been inside the church before. It was not his church; his church was war-shattered and had been closed because the tower was unsafe.

He had been born to the sound of guns. His father had died when the cannons roared. The boy did not know why. His father was not a soldier. He was a quiet man, lame-legged, who could not fight, who tilled the land, and loved his wife and his two small children. Now he was dead.

The boy remembered how his father had knelt at the cradle when the new little sister was born, and looked down on her. He had smiled, and turned his head and seen his son watching, afraid that he had lost his parents' love and was now unwanted. His father had crooked an arm and the boy had come and leaned against the man, and known safety, even though the guns spoke loudly outside, and spoke with venomed tongues.

A month later his father died, tilling the field, caught in the crossfire between two opposing armies fighting a war that the boy did not understand. Only a week after that a bomb had blasted the road where he lived, and the little sister had died. And his home had gone. He watched the flames eat the wood, and saw the charred remains, and his mother had sought in the ruins and found only her rosary and her golden cross, given her long ago by his father. The cross was black with fire.

Nothing had been the same since. They could not even go to the church. And his mother would not go to the other church.

'It is not like ours,' she said.

The boy looked at the church. It differed little from his own. It was very old. Vaulted arches soared towards the sky. The faded carpet on the stone floor stretched towards the altar. The dying sun shone on two silver candlesticks, and on a gleaming crystal cross that hung over an altar cloth faded with time, the colours muted and lovely—dove grey; blue the colour of a rain-washed sky; the delicate rose of a bird's feathered breast; only the tinges of shadows suggested a pattern woven by fingers a long time dead. A breeze from the cracks in the windows shivered the cloth and the cross swayed in the air. In his church a Virgin and Child stood on the altar, and there were pictures on the walls, and Christ died for ever, in agony, on a cross carved by a man who had known such misery. The boy knew the shape of the face and the clenched hands and the knotted muscles in the legs nailed so cruelly to the dark wood. He looked at it, often, wondering.

The boy moved slowly towards the altar. He had had to come. Life was unendurable. His mother had become quiet when his father died; she had ceased, almost, to see him, when his sister was killed. Now she scrubbed floors, doing her work well and saying little, worrying the Sisters who ran the little convent hospital. At night she fed the boy and washed his clothes and mended them, but she did not hear him speak, nor answer him, and when her work was done she sat by the fire and told her rosary over and over, her fingers holding the beads as if they were the only reality left to her. The boy could not find the Father from his own church. But he needed comfort. Perhaps there was comfort here. He did not know. He only knew he had no one to whom he could talk. Perhaps he could talk to God. But was it his God, here, in this strange church?

He had been taught at school a prayer which said *Forgive us our trespasses*. There was a notice in the wood near the village which said *Trespassers will be prosecuted*.

Perhaps God would forgive him for trespassing in a strange church, where there was no Virgin to whom he could pray, and nowhere for him to put his candle. He had taken all the money he had and bought a splendid candle, fat and curved and ridged and beautiful. It would throw a golden light that would soften the darkness, and he would light it for St. Anthony, who found that which was lost.

St. Anthony could not give him back his little sister, or restore his father to him. But new babies were born every day and perhaps his mother could have a new little sister, and she would sing soft lullabies again and laugh, just sometimes. And see him again, and speak to him. He was very much alone. And he was very much afraid. There was one bullet scar on his arm already and he remembered the pain. He did not want that to happen again.

He so hoped that soon there would be no war. No guns. No hatred. The boy once thought that grown-ups knew everything, and were always right, but he was learning fast. They were often wrong. They told untruths and they broke their promises. Perhaps God could help him.

His mother did not understand. 'Go and play, little one,' she said. But how could he play when she was so unhappy and his father and sister were gone, and the frightening guns spoke their messages by day and by night, and he did not know which men were friends and which were enemies? He had thought that Micky's father was a friend, but Micky's father had proved an enemy, coming with his gun, shooting and killing. Yet he had the same face as always. He was still Micky's father, who had played with the boy when he was very small, tickling him, and laughing with his parents and eating food with them. It was not possible to understand.

The church soothed him. He remembered music; the soft sweet singing of boys' voices, as the Aves soared to the sky. It was like the lullaby his mother sang sometimes to the little sister. The baby had listened and her dark eyes had watched, and she had curled her small hands and laughed. She had been sweet, the little sister. Her tiny fingers curled round his big finger and he had felt strong and protective.

'You are a man, now,' his mother said, laughing at him as he lifted the baby from her cradle when it was time for her to feed. That seemed long ago, he thought, when he was young. He was older now. Much older. But he still did not understand.

There was a dog beside the boy; a small brown dog, with merry eyes and lolling tongue and stumpy tail that rarely stopped wagging. The boy had found it among the rubble of a bombed house and brought it home. It had a cut leg and an injured ear, and he had taken it to the hospital where his mother worked and asked one of the Sisters to dress its injuries. She did so, and went with him to a man who cared for animals, and now she sent food home for the dog every night; scraps left over from the hospital meals. The boy loved the dog almost more than anything else in the world. He had so little to love.

At school the teacher had told them the story of Abraham and Isaac; and how a man must sacrifice everything he holds most dear to God, and then perhaps his prayers may be granted. The boy did not know how to make a sacrifice, but perhaps he could give the dog to the Father in this church and God would grant a little sister for his mother, to make her happy again.

He did not know where to put the candle. He was afraid of fire. He could not put it on the altar in case it fell and the beautiful cloth was burned. He walked slowly towards the altar and the dog walked with him, puzzled, but prepared always to follow the boy who had saved it.

The boy did not know how to pray in this church, without candles or a Virgin to look down on him with her serene face and her child held close against her. He put out a finger to touch the faded pattern, a pattern of flying birds and flowers, a memory of a serene past, now long forgotten except for this.

The minister, walking into the church, stared at the child. The minister was an old man, his hair white, his face seamed and saddened. His tired eyes looked out at a world he no longer loved but only grieved for. He spent his days among dying men and women and children, offering what comfort he could, holding a hand here, holding a child tightly, saying over and over, 'Lord, forgive them, for they know not what they do.'

The words were losing meaning. He was beginning to doubt his God. How could men be so stupid, so wicked, so cruel? Where was God? Had he abdicated, hating the men he had created, hoping that his experiment would end, and that the world he had made would return to silence, and to peace, without the beings that peopled it? The minister did not know. He only knew that he was old and no longer understood; that his eyes were sore from the constant tears that filled them; that his throat ached from the need to swallow the pain that his daily work brought; and that his knees were bruised and painful from long contact with the cold stone floor in front of the altar.

He looked down at the child. The minister knew of the child, and of his mother. The Sisters had arranged for them to go across the sea, to another land where they might find peace. The mother was being destroyed by the sound of gunfire. The child did not yet know that he was to make the journey. The light from the window cast brilliance on the small dark head. The minister saw the candle and understood. He was suddenly angry. He did not distinguish between friend and foe. All men were brothers. All men were equal in God's eyes, and in his eyes all men belonged to the same God, no matter what their church said. The child had come for comfort. But how to give it?

He knelt beside the boy and took him gently in his arms. The strong arms closed, and memory betrayed the child so that he felt his own father near him. His thin body shook as tears began. The minister blinked. The tears would ease the hurt.

He took the candle from the boy and walked to the altar. He removed the church candle from its sconce and put the child's offering in its place. He lit the wick and placed the candlestick in the centre of the altar cloth, under the glistening cross. Soft radiance spread over the faded colours of the altar cloth. There were three dark red chrysanthemums in a silver vase beyond the candle. A petal dropped and lay, a scarlet splash of vivid light beneath the cross. It looked like newly shed blood.

The minister prayed. His deep voice filled the church. Darkness shadowed the land outside and gunfire ceased. An owl mocked the silence, and was gone in a feathered sweep of silent wings. The words of comfort flowed on, soothing the child, although he did not understand more than half their meaning. The little dog slept and peace filled the shadows; the candlelight spilled on the altar, and reflected deep in the child's eyes, a minute lambent flame glinting in unfathomable dark.

'It is your turn to pray,' the minister said, hoping that the child would give him a clue that would guide him to future action.

'Can I pray in your church?' the boy asked.

'All churches are God's churches,' the minister said.

The boy closed his eyes. 'Hail Mary, hear me,' he said softly and distinctly. 'I have brought a candle to St. Anthony. Ask him that he make a miracle, with the help of God. Bring me a little sister for my mother to love.'

* * *

They were not alone in the church. There was another man hiding, unseen, lying along one of the pews near the door. The wound that was killing him had bled freely and he knew, with each thudding pump of his heart, that death was coming closer. He prayed that he would not be found by the men who had shot him. He had left a blood trail with his footsteps in the snow. He had come to sanctuary but he did not know if anyone respected God's place in these wicked times. He only knew that he had to come, had to ensure that his last deed on earth was successfully concluded. He had no choice. There was no one else he dared trust. He was like the boy, in that he no longer knew who were his friends and who his enemies.

He needed a miracle and he prayed desperately, and for him there came one. The snow began again, great swirling flakes from a seal-black sky, covering his tracks, hiding the footprints, obliterating the bloodstains, until no mark showed to reveal his coming. He saw the flakes through the broken window, and thanked his God, who was not the God of this church either. But when death came nudging, surely all Gods were the same?

The man wished for absolution, but that was not to be. So he whispered his confession, alone in the dark, and hoped that someone might come and pray with him, that he might not die alone. His mind was clouded and his thoughts were wandering and it was difficult to remember the right words. It was difficult for him to remember anything.

He no longer knew if the cause he fought for was right or wrong. Now, with death only a few heartbeats away, all causes seemed wrong. He had one cause greater than that for which he had fought, and that was why he had come to the church, hoping that God would have pity and solve this last problem for him. It was almost time to sleep. He had never known such weariness. He could hear the sound of the blood dripping from him, drip, drip, drip, on the stone floor. His ears throbbed with the beat of his failing heart, and the church was filled with its noise and with the sonorous words of the man kneeling at the altar.

He heard the boy's words, and tried to call out, but he

could only whisper, and then the minister took up his prayer again. *O God, let there be no more war. Let men live in amity. Let the children know the joys of childhood; the joys so many of them have forgotten. Let them walk beside the little rivers where the frogs spawn in spring; let them pick the cowslips in the green meadows; let them see the summer trees, unmarred by gunshot; let them play children's games in the winter snow. Grant us peace in our time, O Lord.*

'Amen,' said the voice from the back of the church, and the minister and the boy turned startled heads. There was a deep sigh and a sob. A rifle clattered on to the stone floor and the boy jumped up, terrified. The dog snarled. The minister gripped the boy's hand tightly.

'Have no fear,' he said softly. 'We are in God's house now.'

They walked down the shadowy aisle, beyond the circle of light from the candle. They stood looking down at the soldier who had died. He was stretched along the pew, his face peaceful. His uniform was soaked with blood.

The dog whimpered.

'Hush,' the boy said.

'Wait,' the minister said.

He walked back to the altar and brought the candle and held it high. The flame grew tall and swayed and flared in the wind that blew through the cracks in the windows. Snow had drifted in, lying white and soft, glittering silver on the dark stone. The light fell on the boy, reflected deep in the eyes darker than the sky outside, eyes that had seen what the dog had seen, and shone with the realisation of a miracle.

The candle wavered in the age-mottled hand. The flame shone on the carry-cot the dog had found, on the milky skin of the sleeping baby, on the blonde hair that clung, thistledown soft, against the fragile skull. There was an envelope on the white coverlet. The minister did not know if the white was wool or snow. He bent, took the letter and opened it.

There was money inside, a great deal of money, and a hastily written note. *Take her for me*, the soldier had written. *Her mother is dead. She is all I have. Send her away, lest she suffer too. Give my child the chance I cannot give her. God be with you, whoever you are, and thank you.*

'He was an enemy,' the boy said, looking at the stained uniform.

'He was a father, and this is his small daughter,' the minister said.

He closed the blue eyes, and crossed the weathered hands. Tomorrow he would find men to bury the soldier, to bury him quietly, so that no one knew he had come here, or where he lay, or that he had left a child behind him.

'Come,' the minister said. 'We will take the baby to your mother. God has heard your prayer. We will send you all to safety.'

They left the church and walked across the snow. The wind rocked the candle flame and the boy shielded it. St. Anthony had heard his prayer and had made a miracle.

The little dog nosed his leg.

The hardest part was yet to do. But the boy had a trust to perform. He had promised and he would keep his promise even though it meant parting with the creature that he loved almost more than anything else in the world. He looked up at the minister. 'I brought my dog to sacrifice,' he said. 'I cannot kill it, but it is for you.'

The minister paused. He had wrapped the baby in the coverlet and folded his cassock round it. He prayed that no one would see them, that no one would know of the baby. Men were wild, and who knew what they would do if they heard of the soldier's child? Vengeance came easily, with the sharp crack of a gun, and for men like these, knowing neither mercy nor pity, it had no meaning. There were jackals abroad in the dark.

He could not take the dog but he could not refuse the gesture. Then memory came to his aid. 'God released Isaac,' he said. It was a very old story of times as cruel as these. 'Perhaps he will release you too from your bond. Run ahead, my son. If the dog follows you, it will be a sign that you may keep him. If he stays with me, I will keep him. But run. Do not walk, and do not look back.

The boy wanted to pray but he did not. God must decide. He ran, and his footsteps marked the unbroken snow, and the dog, seeing his master speeding away from him, raced to catch him up. The boy knelt, his arms round his dog. He looked up at the minister.

'God has decided. Come,' the old man said, and held out his hand.

He needed yet another miracle. Would the woman accept this child? Or would she turn from it? There were already too many such babes in his care. The orphanage could hold no more, and there was not enough money to feed them all. And the boy needed a sister. He had prayed for a miracle and the miracle had happened. Surely it could not now be spoiled.

His telltale footsteps in the snow worried the minister. He detoured endlessly, watching for snowdrifts, aware of fear walking beside him, knowing himself surrounded by enemies. The snow would muffle their approach. Death might hide behind the hummocked bushes, might speak from the shadowed ditch, might spring from the cow byres.

They turned into the village street. The minister paused and looked about him, hidden by the shadowy corner of a house. The boy waited too, trained to silence, knowing the danger, aware of a horror that happier children would never know. Only his grip on the old man's hand showed his fear.

The dog moved quietly too, knowing from a lifetime of misery that any noise or sudden movement could mean a kick, or a stone flung. He too had long ago learned caution. He kept to heel, and stopped when the minister stopped, and waited for them to move...

The shabby room was quiet. The mother sat by the dying fire, and as they opened the door she turned incurious eyes. She saw the man and the boy, and the dog and the black bundle, and said nothing.

The minister closed the door behind him. The boy set the candle on the table and re-lit the flame. The man uncovered the baby's head and she began to cry, a small, hungry whimpering, a sound of pure exhaustion.

The mother sprang to her feet, her eyes brilliant. She took the child from the man, and looked at him searchingly. 'I have no milk, and no feeding bottle,' she said. 'The child will die.'

'I asked St. Anthony for a baby sister,' the boy said. 'He made a miracle.'

'I will bring you what you need from the orphanage,' the minister promised. 'Will you keep the child? Her father is dead. I must return soon and bury him before his killers find that he lived long enough to reach the church and to save his child.'

'I will keep the baby,' the woman said. 'My son asked for a miracle, and she came. It is a sign.'

The boy lifted the candle. The soft glow cast a radiance over the bare shabby room and gilded the baby's head. The dog drank, lapping noisily, and the woman held the child as if afraid she might lose it again. The baby turned her head and saw the golden cross against the woman's throat. Her small hand clutched at it and she smiled.

'I will come back with food for her, and for you and the boy,' the minister said.

Candlelight glinted on the boy. Brilliance shone from his eyes. There was a smile on his lips as he watched the baby play with the cross. The woman held the tiny head close against her, and held out her other hand to the boy. 'I have two children now,' she said, looking from her son's tanned face to the delicate creamy baby. She turned to the minister. 'I will keep both of them safe, Father,' she said.

The snow had ceased when he stepped outside. Far away, his church glittered in the moonlight, its scars hidden. Its spire soared out towards the star-studded sky, glittering and perfect, under a moon that was a slender crescent in a vault of midnight blue. Long dark shadows from the trees round the churchyard cast their bars across the glistening land.

The minister looked up. 'Give us peace in our time, O Lord,' he murmured softly. The woman had come to the door of the house. She too looked at the stars. 'Father, tell me,' she said. 'If there were no war, would we value peace?'

He looked at her; she was a shadow among the other shadows, the child cradled against her.

He had no answer. He did not know.

THE UNINVITED ONE

'No more dogs,' Mark said, when Tara died.

I agreed. I couldn't bear that again. Tara had been part of our lives for nearly fifteen years. She was a cross breed, some Alsatian, some collie, a beautiful bitch with gentle ways. She had slept by my bed, and when Mark was away it was good to put down a hand and be rewarded by that lifted nose, and a swift lick that banished aloneness.

I couldn't bear the house without her.

I turned when the wind blew the curtains, when a faint sound whispered in another room. I expected to see her in the corner behind my chair, her brown eyes watching me, longing for me to put down my work and pick up her lead, and go out.

There were reminders of her everywhere.

I couldn't face a puppy. Not with four meals a day, and puddles to correct, and the long teaching. Tara had needed so little attention for the past years. She knew our ways; she knew when she had to be quiet; she knew when to bark; she protected me on the lonely walks that I took, that were not so lonely with her beside me, nudging my knee, her eyes saying 'Look, rabbit!'

Now it was lonelier than ever. Mark was an executive in a very new firm that was beginning to make its way in the exporting of craftmade woollen goods. The knitwear was supplied by crofters' wives; beautiful handmade shawls and stoles; crocheted dresses and suits; patterned jerseys; even a wedding dress, gossamer fine, intricately patterned in a design of roses and leaves, made by an old woman living on a remote Hebridean island, putting the work of many of the younger ones to shame.

The demand could not be met. Mark travelled to find new workers and then travelled to sell the goods. I sometimes felt I had married a ghost. A man who appeared in my life briefly, filled the house with life and laughter, and vanished again, leaving it dead.

Deader than ever without Tara.

We had only one daughter.

Anna was away at college. I couldn't burden her with my loneliness. She was eighteen. Life was just beginning and life was tremendous fun. She came home as briefly as her father, made me laugh and filled the empty rooms, and then she went and the house was quieter than ever.

I thought about another dog. But a dog was a tie, no two ways about that. I could go away. But where could I go, alone? I had so few friends left and most of them were working. I had my own job, but I worked at home, writing cookery books, trying out new recipes, sometimes entertaining, but more often than not my meals were solitary and it was hardly surprising that my best seller was titled *Meals For One*.

Summer passed.

I rarely walked now. There was little point. Autumn came with a wild blustering. Anna had been home and gone again. Mark was touring the States, full of excitement because he was finding so many new markets. Some of the clothes he took with him were gorgeous. He had given me one of the lacy shawls. The work was so fine that it reminded me of a long-forgotten fairy tale about a princess who wanted a wedding dress so delicate that it could be pulled through her mother's wedding ring. Cobweb soft, beautiful.

I wasn't living.

I was just existing, going on from day to day, pointlessly. I walked through the silent rooms. I woke, and washed, and dressed, and tidied the house, and wrote. The only sound was the swiftly ticking clock, ticking my life away; ticking the hours till Mark came home, or Anna phoned; her 'hey, Mum' brightened the dreary day.

Late at night I heard a whine.

I looked out of the window. A dog was sitting in the garden, looking up at the lighted window. A small cross-bred dog that reminded me of Tara, yet was nothing like Tara. The brown eyes watched the window. I went outside and the dog vanished in the bushes. I whistled, but it did not come.

I wondered about it, lost and lonely, out there in the stormy night. In the morning I found pawmarks all over the garden and the dustbin overturned and the rubbish strewn around.

I glimpsed the dog again briefly that afternoon. We lived in a lonely road, in a lonely house, the nearest neighbour within sight, but not within sound. I had loved the house when Anna was small. I had never felt isolated then. Now somehow the marauding dog made me feel much more isolated. Suppose I met it in the dark? Suppose it were savage? Suppose it attacked me?

I felt unnerved.

Yet, every night when I went to draw the curtains, the dog was there, sitting on the lawn, watching the house. As soon as I went outside, it ran away.

I began to watch for it, to feel cheated if the garden were empty. I began to put out food. I still had Tara's plate; her bed and her blankets, tucked away, not wanting to get rid of them, not wanting to cast away my last links with her. Her picture stood on the mantelpiece. The last thing I saw at night was the look in her wise eyes. Sometimes I thought I ought to put the picture away, but that would have been betrayal.

The dog came regularly.

I began to put the food down and stay outside, waiting. I soon realised this wasn't a dog, but a bitch. What was more, she was in milk. I began to worry, to wonder where the pups were, to wonder who had cast her out to forage on her own. She was a pretty little animal, daintily made, collie cross on something smaller, perhaps a corgi, brown and white and black, with a broad wise face and wide ears that flopped on either side of her head.

She began to come closer, to approach cautiously, and

when she had fed, she wagged her tail, but as soon as I moved towards her, she ran off, jumping the low garden wall, and vanished on the moor.

I watched for her coming; watched the empty heather stretches, watched the side of the burn, and saw that she always came by the same track, an old track made by other beasts, perhaps by foxes, perhaps by deer. There were deer too sometimes, out there in the dark, stealing my flowers, eating succulently for once.

Mark came home, but I did not tell him about the bitch. I put her food out before we went to bed, and I knew that she came. He went again, and we resumed our old routine, a pattern that had endured for nearly four weeks.

Late one night, after I had gone to bed, I heard a whimper at the back door. I went downstairs. The autumn night had become bitterly cold. There was frost glittering in the moonlight, patterning the bushes, white on the grass. There was no sign of the bitch, but there was a small whimpering bundle on the doorstep that was soaking wet and very cold.

I took him in, and switched on the fire and found towels and rubbed him dry. He was black and white, and fluffy, and might have been almost any breed. He nosed my finger hungrily.

There was a scratch at the door and another whimper. And again there was a small bundle, wet and freezing, tucked against the door. I wondered how many pups she had. I wondered if she would bring them all to me. I stopped wondering when I heard her arrive with a third member of her family. I was elected to help her. She trusted me. She knew the cold could kill, and she knew that houses meant warmth and food.

By four in the morning I had five puppies warming by the fire. The bitch was sitting on the doorstep with a sixth in her mouth twenty minutes later. I heard her urgent paw. When I opened the door she walked in, and settled by the fire, and licked him. She was cold herself, but she nosed the pups into the centre of the hearth rug, basking in the heat by the fire, and suckled them.

When the pups were fed, she left them. They were

about five weeks old. They could run unsteadily, and for a few minutes they played and rolled and bit at one another. I brought all the newspapers I had and spread them on the floor, and laid the pups on the paper. The bitch watched, bright-eyed, well aware that I was ready to help.

She followed me into the kitchen, and allowed me to rub her dry. She let me stroke her head, and praise her and pet her and then she fed, eating everything on the plate. She went back to lie among the pups, and I left her and went upstairs to sleep, happily aware that the house was no longer empty and that I had a new interest, even if it were both arduous and embarrassing, and would bring problems.

The problems were less than I expected. I found an old wooden box and cleaned it, and lined it with blankets. I named the bitch Shona. She learned her name at once, and soon was mine, coming to me eagerly, expecting me to help her and play with her pups. She brought them to me when she fed them, dropping each one in my lap, sure it would be given a royal welcome.

I rang the vet, who came and was amazed at the strength of the puppies. Shona had been living wild for weeks, yet they were as healthy as any carefully bred pups. He gave me a diet sheet and I soon found myself weaning them, while Shona, tired of maternal responsibility, dodged the urgent mouths, and escaped from the pups at night by coming up to sleep beside my bed.

The pups were sold, for a pittance, as my vet said that nobody appreciated anything that came free. I charged just enough to cover the cost of their food while I had had them. Shona stayed with me. No one admitted to having lost her. No one answered the advertisement I put in the paper.

Mark laughed when he saw the litter.

'She knew where to come,' he said. 'She knew better than we did. We need a dog. It must be lonely here when Anna and I are both away. You never lived here without Tara.'

We had moved when Anna was three. Tara was seven months old.

Shona licked his hand.

Life's fun again. Long walks and wild romps and a muzzle lifted to lick my wrist at night, and no more aloneness when Mark is away. The vet says she is about two years old. I whistle and she comes to me, tail wagging, body wriggling, delighted to be wanted. And I am delighted too. I need Shona as much as she needs me. Now I must stop and take her for her walk and as I turn and look at Tara's picture I see approval in her eyes. I have an odd feeling that Tara sent the bitch to me, knowing I cannot live without a dog. Knowing I would never have the courage to buy a pup and supplant her memory. Shona has made the memory kind and laid my little ghost.

THE SHOEBLACK ON THE PONT NEUF

Nobody ever knew his name. It is possible he had forgotten it himself, as he had never belonged to anyone in his life, not that he could remember. They called him Jacques, and he ran barefoot with the other boys, and listened to the aftermath of the wars that had torn Europe, and to rumours of revolution, and he learned to read the numbers on the papers that told the date.

The years went by, and he learned that to survive he must have a trade; but who would sponsor a barefoot boy from the Paris slums? A boy who lived under the arches, sleeping where he could, knowing very little other than the need to snatch food and run away and stay alive, dodging the galloping hooves of the many horses drawing the vehicles over the muddy cobbled streets.

He found he could make a little money by helping old Marcel, who plied his brushes in a corner near the Pont Neuf. Sometimes he was allowed to black the shoes of the less important customers, who were glad to have the mud and horse dung removed from their footwear before going on to an appointment.

Most of their customers were officers from the big barracks over the way.

Jacques was in awe of them. He was small, deprived of growth by his poor diet and haphazard way of life. He learned to duck the angry cuffs of those who bullied him, and he found that the only friends he could make were among the many dogs that roamed the streets, fighting him for food that the rich had flung from their doorways. He could not imagine how it felt to have so much to eat that you could throw it away.

He spent his spare time teaching one of the many mongrels that roved along the banks of the Seine; he taught him all kinds of little tricks that they sometimes performed together beside the long theatre queues, earning laughter and approval. Jacques had a quick monkey smile that endeared him to the crowds.

Then Marcel died, with only Jacques to nurse him in his last hours, and he bequeathed his only possession to the boy. At last Jacques had a trade; he had status and a place to belong, for now he was the shoeblack on the corner of the Pont Neuf and he earned enough to buy himself a bed in a back room in a broken-down house and a little food to eat.

By day he was haunted, around the year 1815, by a large and friendly poodle pup. Jacques did not know that this was a pedigree dog, that had been stolen for ransom, and had escaped, and come at last in its wanderings to Paris. The dog, which he named Chien, not being very original in his thoughts, attached himself to the shoeblack, who had a lonely place in his life that badly needed filling.

He rescued the pup from boys who threw stones and men who kicked, and took it home with him. It slept on the floor by his bed, guarded his daily takings against sneak thieves, and Jacques taught it many tricks. The dog was clever and loved learning and was lucky in having found a master that loved teaching.

The dog learned to carry the brushes and the dusters; to come when he was called, to sit by his master's side; and to beg with appealing eyes, especially when anyone passed with food in his hand, or in her shopping bag.

Many ladies whose shoes were not in need of cleaning stopped to have them dusted and to stroke the big friendly animal, and reward him with a titbit. Some came daily, bringing dainties for the dog, which Jacques shared without remorse, as he saw to it that Chien never went hungry, even when he himself had little enough for food.

Gradually there built up an understanding between man and dog. Chien would sit, head raised, eyes on his master, speaking with every glance, asking for time for a stroke, for the brushes to be put away, for one of their long walks beside the river.

Most of the day Jacques had only time to look out over the river, to look towards the spires of Notre Dame, to look up at the clouded sky, and to look down at the water slipping endlessly under the bridge, busy with boats carrying wares to places all over the world, remote and undreamed-of places that were only names to him, sometimes described by the sailors who drank with him in the taverns and spoke of far-off lands, and of England, across the channel, always so grey and cold, and Ireland, where many men were even poorer than Jacques himself, and there was often famine.

He looked at Chien, lying innocently beside him, now sound asleep, quite unaware of the worry he caused. Business was poor, and the shoeblack was hungry and an idea was slowly forming in his head. He had been afraid he might have to sell the dog.

He packed up his brushes into the little satchel, and whistled to the dog, who bounded eagerly, overjoyed to discover that today was a red-letter day; a playing instead of a work day, something that very rarely happened, as the people on their way to church on Sundays might well stop to have their shoes dusted on a dry hot day, or the mud removed on a wet day.

Chien and his master walked a long way that day to a private stretch of beach, where the dog could swim and roll. When he was muddy, the shoeblack called to him, encouraging him to roll against his master's legs, which Chien did with fervour. He was patted and praised, and rewarded with all the food that the man had in his bag, and the lesson was repeated.

They were on duty at dawn next day.

The shoeblack took Chien into the water, and waited until the first pair of shining boots appeared in his sight. He nudged the dog and whispered.

'Roll!'

Chien sped off, sure that he would be rewarded once he had done as he was told. He wagged his tail, greeting the stranger, a fierce old man on his way to open the bank nearby.

The dog rolled, dirtying the spotless shoes.

He sat, mouth agape, grinning, as the old man swore violently and tried to kick the dog. Chien ran off, to hide himself until it was safe to return. The shoeblack ignored him, polished the shoes until they shone like mirrors and tutted with the old man, agreeing that the dog was the son of the devil and its owner should be consigned to the Bastille.

The fee for shoeblacking that morning was trebled. Chien learned very fast. He learned to roll on the shiniest shoes; and he learned to race off as if he belonged elsewhere, so that no one realised he was in fact the shoeblack's dog. Those who did know were spared from Chien's attentions. After all, they were customers already. Chien never rolled twice on the same man.

The shoeblack prospered. He was able to afford a better room and more food. He replaced his brushes and polishes, and began to be well-known among the young officers from the barracks. Even the important officers, older men with arrogant manners, pompous and proud, sometimes stopped for a shoeshine. The shoeblack knew better than to send the dog to roll on them. They might have Chien shot and lose him a considerable source of income and pleasure. By now he and the dog were inseparable and could read each other's minds; there was time to spend on Sunday afternoons walking in public gardens, where Chien could run and play the fool and exert his own authority. No dog ever challenged Chien. He was top dog among the delicate pets in the parks and they all recognised the fact.

When Chien was five years old an officer from England came to stay in Paris. When the dog rolled on him he was angry, but his anger died when he saw his gleaming shoes. He walked to the end of the bridge, and looked down on the boats; and looked around him, savouring the city. He had never been abroad before and there was a shine on Paris that he would never see again, as he would see it through experienced eyes.

Everything fascinated him.

The buildings here were splendid, fronting the river, reminding him of his own busy Thames. The shoeblack worked for some time, and then the officer saw the dog swim in the river and roll in the mud, and lumber up the bank. He watched, intrigued, and saw a smart young captain stride towards the shoeblack.

He also saw the shoeblack give a swift signal with his hand. The dog raced over to the captain and rolled on his shoes. The often-repeated scene was enacted again; the anger; the oaths; the swift kick that Chien avoided, running off, tail between his legs, the picture of guilt, to hide under an archway while the shoeblack worked busily to remedy the damage.

That was quite a dog.

The young English officer waited until the captain had gone and went to talk to the shoeblack.

'That's a very clever dog you have,' he said.

'My dog, monsieur?' The man was not going to admit that this was his dog. Anxious brown eyes stared upwards into the officer's face.

'Sell me the dog, and I won't tell. I'll give you ten English sovereigns for him.'

Ten sovereigns was a fortune. But the shoeblack did not want to sell his dog.

'If I tell the officers at the barracks about him, he'll be shot. As it is many of them are very angry with him,' the Englishman said.

Chien left with the Englishman, tied ignominiously by a rope, which was replaced later with a collar and lead. The dog was bathed, and brushed, a procedure that he hated. Within ten days he was on his way to England, a handsome dog, very much admired by everybody.

But he was a miserable dog, hating the change in his life, refusing food, hankering for the freedom of the river and the free and easy life he had known before; never leashed, but running wild, dodging excitedly among the horses' hooves, chasing after cats and pigeons, barking without being scolded.

Now he had to learn not to bark at cats and birds and to sit quietly when his new master was busy. He had to learn to answer commands in a strange language. His new master wondered if the dog were dull, not realising that a dog that had answered to the name Chien all his life, spoken in a French accent, could not understand the same name when spoken by an English tongue. It sounded like Cheyenne and meant nothing to him. Nor did SIT when he had been used to Assis!

His new life bored him. Much of the time he was shut away; he spent hours at night in a kennel, instead of lying beside his master on the tumbled bed. He was taught new ways, and taught harshly, as the Englishman was sure the dog was stubborn and did not realise how much the change of life and language had upset him.

One day Chien found the door of his kennel open and he slipped away.

His nose led him to the river. Rivers were familiar and so were boats. This river was the Thames. He loped beside it until it became a large river, and he found that he could pick up some of his old life again, chasing cats and barking at pigeons and scavenging in the gutters.

He preferred hunting for his own food. He had not cared for the diet given him by his new master.

He spent some months by the river. Then, late one night, lying with his nose on his paws, watching the moon rise over the trees, he heard a drunken man singing a familiar song. A French song. There were words and phrases that brought echoes of another life to his mind.

He followed the man.

Chien had travelled to England on a boat. He had hated it, but this boat would take him back to Paris. He was quite certain that where there were Frenchmen there would be home. He ran aboard and was greeted with amusement by the crew, who decided to adopt him as a mascot, especially as he responded joyfully to French commands.

Chien wanted only to go home.

As soon as the boat reached Marseilles he jumped ashore, and, although the men called to him and tried to bring him back, he was soon lost in the crowds. His nose told him the way. He had an inbuilt instinct inside him that drove him relentlessly, stopping only to forage for food.

It was easy to find food in the country; on the waste heaps on the farms, outside the cottages, in the yards of all the shopkeepers. Chien fed very well. Many of the people who saw him tried to make him stay, but he had no time for them.

He had only one enormous need.

To reach Paris.

The shoeblack missed his dog. Business was good, but it wasn't the same and he had had a sneaking sense of amusement at seeing the dog muddy the fine gentlemen whom he sometimes despised with their foppery and superiority and artificial ways. They knew nothing about life. Most of them knew nothing about war either. He did respect the veterans, but these young fellows still wet behind the ears, patronising and superior, what did they know?

He had plenty of time to think, and no one to talk to, now his dog was gone. He had not even spent the money, feeling it was blood money and he as bad as Judas for selling his only friend.

Dawn was brightening the river one rainy morning. The shoeblack was waiting, more lonely than ever, as the people began to stir. Women, calling to him as they hurried off to jobs in the houses and markets; men jollying one another, and ignoring him.

He took a croissant from his satchel. He had not eaten croissants for days as business had lagged, but yesterday there had been a big dinner in the house across the river and some of the guests had walked, as it was a fine day. There was money to spare, as he cleaned the dusty shoes.

The food was snatched from his hand.

Furious, the shoeblack turned to swear and there was Chien, bolting down the dainty, before coming to his master, wagging his tail, rolling in ecstasy, groaning with the delight of being back, of being home, of reunion.

The shoeblack could not speak. He could only hug his dog, and pat his dog, and exclaim over and over again, astounded at seeing him again.

Chien was muddy and wet, but who cared?

An officer came striding over the bridge, swinging his swagger stick and whistling.

Chien did not wait for a command. He flew at the man and rolled.

There was a yell and a shout of fury. Chien fled from the kick that was aimed at him and the shoeblack, composing a face that was aching to laugh, began to lay out his brushes.

That night he spent money on food for himself and the dog; and gave the change to St Anthony, who finds lost things and restores them to their owners.

The Englishman was not too sad; the purchase had been a mistake and the dog would never have settled. The man supposed the dog was dead, lost and starving somewhere in England until some accident ended his life.

He never guessed that the dog was back in Paris, maddening officers from the barracks over the bridge while the shoeblack, his life once more complete, whistled and sang as he worked, and rewarded the most important creature in his world with meat, every single night, raw juicy bones, which always were bought before the man's own food.

Chien revelled in life again.

He was home, even if home were only a garret room and the streets round the bridge in the most exciting city in the world.

In time he was as well-known as his master and those who knew him laughed when he rolled against them, and brought titbits for him, and were sad when he was an old dog lying in the sun, wagging his tail gaily, but no longer able to muddy their boots.

THE INHERITORS

There was nothing left but memory as Trant lay and watched the Eden they had created. The plains rolled in front of him, fair and free, to the far blue dimness that was the horizon. Behind him, the same vista stretched to the belt of new trees that thrust eagerly skywards, drinking in rain and sunshine, bringing promise with each new spring.

Fifty of them had weathered the war that shattered the world. Now only he was left, left with bitter memory, and yet with a hint of a future that would be immeasurably better than anything Earth had known. Perhaps, in distant days, the men who had fled to the stars would return, and find here solace, and a glimpse of paradise, unblemished.

Soon he would die, and he was not sorry. The last year had been too lonely, without another voice to speak to him, without a hand that could reach out and shake his, thrusting away fear and isolation, without another human creature in sight.

They had hoped for so much, the fifty of them, immured in the deep earth, while the bombs rained from the satellites that straddled the sky. They had planned for this time, had vast stores that would last them until their instruments showed that the air was fit to breathe, had studied every contingency, taken every precaution, until nothing could possibly go wrong.

The vast underground caverns had been turned into a town. Here were stores that would last for a century, here was fuel for the machines, and the tiny jet planes themselves that were to quarter the world, bringing succour, were also hidden. Those who found the long days of imprisonment intolerable visited the hangars where they waited, and found fresh hope.

Here were the vast refrigerators which held medical supplies and seeds; the byres where the cattle lived in eternal lamplight; the pens for sheep and styes for pigs, and the stables for the horses. It was good to have the animals to tend, to have lambs and foals and calves to rear, and watch them playing, unaware that up above was a place where the sun still shone.

When the time had gone, and the air was fit again, the fifty men emerged. They could not stand the light for long, nor the scenes of devastation. Earth had returned to the primitive, a gashed heap of scarred rock and maimed mountains, a place of chaos.

Beyond them were the other buried towns; those where the nurseries had been, and the womenfolk, each isolated, each well primed, knowing just what to do, just how to survive. But the turrets stayed shut, and the men went to investigate.

The towns were catacombs, where machinery had been twisted and torn by earth faults that sent the shudders of bombs deep into the ground, and fractured the pipes that brought oxygen. Women and children were gone.

The jets scoured the cities of the world, and everywhere found the same story. Only fifty men had survived. The days of man upon Earth were numbered.

Some were hopeless, and gave up the struggle to keep alive, but the planners, the thinkers, the doctors, the scientists, could not bear to think of a planet denuded when they could bring life of a kind again.

Grimly, they set to work, finding the biggest flat area available, far out in the old savannah lands, where new rivers flowed, bringing nourishment to the thirsty land.

They ploughed, they sowed, they planted. The inventions that man had left behind him, to speed growth, to quicken the spread of grass and clover, so that ground cover was swift and fantastically efficient, all these they used.

The slow years went by, their numbers growing fewer as the old left them, and the young ones aged, and worked on in grim futility, not wishing to end life once and for all, yet wondering to what purpose they laboured.

The sun rose and set on a world that became green again. So little had survived. No more weeds, only the grass and flowers that man planted, so that dahlias bloomed at the edge of the savannah and buttercups were unknown.

The trees shot skywards, graceful, uncrowded, their crowns yielding shade from a sun that seemed hotter than before. The few birds that had been treasured were released to breed among the branches, and they bred quickly, untroubled by hawk or eagle, by rat or weasel, or hunting owl.

The sheep and cattle were brought to the savannah, and bred, and wandered far afield, becoming wild in habit, yet unafraid, for there was no gun to harry them, nor any wild beast. Nor did man trouble them. It seemed a shame to kill the few beasts that lived, and there were stores enough to last until the end of man's time.

And now it was come. A year ago Rivers had dropped as he worked, and Trant had buried him, digging the soft earth and murmuring prayers that had lost all meaning. It was so hard to remember a time when words had had meaning, for Rivers had been dumb with shock since the day that had revealed to them that they indeed were the last inhabitants of Earth.

Trant raised his head. He was tired, and thirsty, but he could not even lift his hand, nor bring the cup to his mouth. He looked at it now, a clay cup, made as the ancient man had made their drinking vessels, for nothing of civilisation had survived, except for the stored food, and the seeds that were now being blown to sow the world.

Eden stretched before him. The peaceful cattle grazed, and even as the westering sun touched his face with its last warmth, he saw the wild horses raise their heads and run, manes rising and falling, lithe bodies racing in flying beauty, every movement the epitome of grace.

He died. And the world was new again, and young again, and the inheritors of peace grazed, unafraid, for killing had gone from their world. The beasts of man inherited Paradise, and the despoiler was gone, for ever.

CAGED

The zoo was waking to life. Inside their cages the lions paced and roared, urgently asking for food. Tera, the Bengal tiger, turned his lithe body, pacing the cage again and again.

Myra took up her bucket and went down the long, stone-floored passage, smiling. She knew what would happen as she came near.

She stopped to listen. She heard the swift patter of tiny, clawed feet, and the sound of urgent whimpers. Tavi was hungry and was telling her fiercely that he needed food.

She went into the passage between the cages, clanging the iron door behind her. Now she could see Tavi through the grille. He had left his water-tank and was running excitedly along the hot-water pipes, now and again leaping to the ground and standing on his hind legs, uttering shrill, excited cries.

Myra chuckled. She took the fish and piled it into her bucket. Tavi would be greedy for it, and she enjoyed feeding the little Malayan otter. When he was fed she could stroke him and pet him, but now he was fierce and eager to eat.

She flung the fish through the bars, and he seized it, standing over it to eat, watching her distrustfully with his sliding eyes.

She never tired of admiring the shining pelt, his sleek body, which he groomed like a cat, and his grace in the water.

He finished his meal and came to her, diving cleanly across the water so that the silver drops showered over her green overall. She rubbed them off, laughing.

Tavi dived again, shooting through the water and coming up on the surface to grab his ball. Myra had bought it for him—a big, gaily-coloured child's ball, and she was surprised to find how much he loved it.

He played with it endlessly, lying on his back, holding it in his paws and flinging it into the air and catching it, so that often he collected quite a crowd round his cage.

Now he flung it up twice to please her, and then, full fed, he climbed out of the water and began to make his way across to the warm corner beneath the pipes where he liked to sleep.

Half-way there he paused, and suddenly whimpered—an eerie, horrible noise that surprised Myra, for it was completely new to him.

She thought that perhaps the fish she had given him was bad, and had given him a pain, and she watched him, concerned, as he squatted on his haunches, staring over her shoulder, still crying dismally.

Then Myra turned, and her face whitened. Tera, the Bengal tiger, stood between her and the door, which had slammed shut behind him. His striped body was arched and his tail waved to and fro, again and again, lashing angrily, and a deep growl snarled in his throat.

Tavi had moved again, and now cowered against the wall, his small body trembling, his nose twitching. The smell of tiger was so strong that Myra felt overwhelmed by it, and was suddenly aware that the animal-house was filled with terror.

The giraffes in the end cage cowered against the wall, unable to hide or run, remembering the smell of lion and tiger, remembering the terror of the wild that made them speed through the long grass, seeking sanctuary.

The zebras squealed in terror and kicked their heels against the wall of their cage. The noise distracted Tera, infuriated him, and he sprang, snarling, against the iron bars that shook to his onslaught but did not give.

Myra stared along the passage. She, too, had nowhere to run or hide. If she could only get through the iron door and lock it, the tiger would be trapped in the passage. But he was nearer the door than she, and she knew that if she moved suddenly he would be upon her.

Again he hurled himself against the zebra cage, and the

animals backed against the wall, still screaming in terror, kicking against one another, provoking him with their din.

Perhaps she could get to the door while he was distracted.... But before she had time to try, he turned and began to advance towards her, giving one last, angry roar at the terrified zebras.

Myra pressed against the otter's cage, and found herself leaning against the little grille that opened to let the men in to clean the cage. This was only done when the otter was safely in his sleeping quarters, and these, at the moment, were sealed off for repairs, as water had leaked in through the roof.

But there was no other hope. If Tavi bit her, at least it would not be so bad as Tera's mauling. She opened the grille, leaped through and slammed it shut.

The tiger gave a roar of fury and hurled his weight against the cage. Tavi hissed furiously, and Myra watched with a sinking heart as the bars shook.

Tera roared in baffled fury. Then he charged again, and the little otter, suddenly stimulated to action, raced across the cage and flung himself into the water-tank, so that the water splashed out in deep, foaming gushes, soaking the infuriated tiger, who retreated and sat down, like an angry cat, to lick himself dry.

Myra looked at the tank. Perhaps she, too, could distract the tiger. For the moment he was busy, but she felt sure that the lull would not last.

Help must be coming. He could not possibly have escaped without someone knowing. The noise from this house must soon attract attention. Meanwhile, there was little she could do.

Tavi came towards her and she eyed him warily. She often spoke to him and stroked him through the bars, but she had never before ventured into his cage, and he might resent her presence.

She did not move as he sniffed at her shoes. Then he lifted his head and hissed at her with pleasure.

She remembered that her hands still smelled of fish, and she was grateful. He licked at her, and then, quite happy in her presence, leaned against her legs.

There was a pause that seemed endless. The tiger paced restlessly up and down, maddened by the smell of prey so close. Then rage possessed him. He leaped at the zebras' and the otter's cage, roaring with fury, and Myra watched in horror as the bars shook at each fresh onslaught.

The bars of her own cage threatened to buckle before the massive body of the great beast. They were not meant to withstand so great an animal.

She watched the sunlight barring his striped body, saw the smooth head and whiskers and deceptive tabby-cat face that broke into ferocity, and then, as he charged again, she used both hands to hurl water into his face.

He backed away and shook himself, brushing one paw again and again over his eyes like a fireside tabby, hating to get wet. Myra was ready to use her one weapon again when she heard the outside door clang.

Tera roared loudly.

"Be careful!" she shouted, as loudly as she could, and the tiger, maddened by the sound of her voice, hurled at the bars, which crashed inwards at his onslaught.

The otter gave a yicker of dismay and hurled himself into her arms. The tiger recovered his balance and crouched, preparing to spring.

Myra shut her eyes and waited for the rending jaws. . . . And then she heard a shot, followed by a last despairing roar.

The sound echoed throughout the animal-house. The zebras beat demented hooves against the wall, the giraffes trembled and shook, and the otter burrowed deep into Myra's arms as she crouched against the wall.

She opened her eyes. The tiger lay dead on the floor, and the other keepers were crowding in excitedly about her, helping her to her feet.

Tavi hissed in fury as they touched her. His sharp teeth opened in a silent snarl, ready to bite, and the men backed away.

Myra laughed shakily and walked out, avoiding the striped body that would, she was sure, haunt her dreams for months to come. She moved to put the little otter in the empty cage next door, but he would not leave her.

Laughing, she went out with him still in her arms.

Many people used to wonder at Myra's pet, a little otter that lived in a cage in her bathroom and spent hours playing in her bath. But they all turned faces of blank disbelief upon her when she explained that the otter refused to leave her since he'd saved her from a tiger.

DROUGHT

There had never been a summer like it.

The sun burned down, day after day, from a sky that had forgotten rain. The grass was burnt in the parched fields. The cattle, ribs showing, eyes staring, swayed in the relentless heat, and gave no milk.

The little pigs sickened and died.

Water was rationed. Only from six until eight in the morning could they fill the buckets, and take water to the troughs. After that, the taps were dry.

The river was only a memory. The clay was mottled and barred, and cracked and hard. There was a shallow pool in the centre of the lake, which was scummed and foul.

The world had narrowed to a few dry fields; to a herd of dying cattle; to endless work, so that hands were blistered and sore from carrying metal handles that held the sun, and burned dry skin.

Not even nightfall brought peace, for the nights were hot, and lightning flickered continuously, and thunder rumbled ominously. Yet no drop of rain fell.

There were mirages on the fields. Clear cool water lying in the hollows, blue as the summer sun. The farmer and his wife ran to them. They vanished, without a trace, leaving only a memory and another beckoning lake in the far distance.

The farmer grew thin and gaunt and angry. His temper

flickered with the lightning. Unable to rail at his God, he railed at his wife, searing her with his tongue, as the sun seared the fields.

There was only one sanctuary.

There was water for just one hour every morning; and her spirit broke. One night, as the sun vanished in a long flare of red, she walked barefoot to the little church.

She was a small woman, made smaller by her weariness. Her shoulders bowed, aching, from the constant carrying of buckets; from the constant need to bury the dying animals; from the constant fear that their troubles were driving her man mad.

She stood inside the doorway.

The lamp burned at the feet of the carved Madonna, with her serene face, and with her child cradled against her. She was the essence of peace; the reminder of a time long ago when the farmer's wife had been a child and had leaned against her father's strength on such a night as this.

He had held her close when the storm raged, and comforted her, and told her there was nothing to fear. She longed for him now.

She longed to be a child again, and unaware of adult woes.

She put out her finger, and traced the pattern of Mary's robe. It was etched in dust. She took her handkerchief and tried to clean the statue. The lamp burned low. The shadows moved. The lightning flashed four times on the walls.

And then came darkness.

The farmer's wife knelt and crossed herself.

Should the lightning kill her, she would die in front of her God.

Holy Mary, have pity on us, for we are miserable sinners.

Father, forgive them, for they know not what they do. Forgive my man, for the drought is driving him mad, and I cannot help him.

The whole town feared the drought and feared the storm and longed for rain. Children cried fretfully, tossing off clinging sheets that were damp against small bodies. Parents, wakeful, made cups of tea, careful with the water, and watched the flickering sky.

A police car prowled slowly along lamplit streets, windows wide, the men, sweltering, sitting in shirt sleeves, watching the shadows fly before them, banished by the headlights' glare.

They passed the other church, where the vicar of the parish kept his own vigil. He was an old man, white-haired, thin-faced, and so kind that the suffering of his parishioners was a constant torment. He feared for the world in which he lived. Fire and flood; famine and earthquake; war, and men who found a high pleasure in killing, born with bloodlust that was worse than that of the beasts of the jungle, for they only killed to eat and live.

He was afraid of the ceaseless flickering light beyond the town, over the bare moors; it lighted the town.

There was a rustle in the church.

A rat fled along the pews and vanished down a hole. The vicar hated rats.

There were rats in the other church too. The heat had brought them out of the ground in search of water. The farmer's wife saw the sudden scurry and the wicked eyes, and the twisting tail, and went out into the night, afraid now of her own church.

She needed company, but she did not know where to find it.

There were lights in the other church. She walked towards it, head bowed, afraid of the night; afraid of the scorching sun; afraid of her own frailty. She hesitated at the lighted door, but her need for companionship was great.

She went inside.

The church was austere. Bare white walls, and high arched ceiling, with pillars that soared out of sight, hidden by shadows. The altar was covered in a white cloth, and on it was a silver crucifix. The vicar turned his head and smiled at her, welcoming her, although he had never seen her before.

Behind her, shadowy, came a cat. The cat was thirsty too. He lived wild, part of a factory at the edge of the town, but the men had so little water now that they had forgotten the cat. It was a large tabby; it came to the vicar and purred and rubbed against his legs.

It leaped to the font and drank.

The woman gasped, thinking this sacrilege. She would have chased the animal out of the church, but the old man smiled at her again.

"Even the fall of a sparrow," he said softly. "Would God deny a little cat a drink of water?"

There was no sound in the church but the soft lapping.

The cat leaped to the ground and weaved between the old man's legs, while light flashed on the white-washed walls, splashed through the stained-glass windows, bathing the altar in blood; flared on the pews and the lectern.

The old man knelt.

Our father, who art in heaven . . .

The woman whispered softly under her breath.

Mary, have mercy upon us, for we are miserable sinners.

The cat crept between the old man, and the farmer's wife, glad of company. They kept vigil together in the dusty church. Dust motes danced in the candle beams.

Out on the moors a young fox was dreaming of water. Water, clear and cool, sparkling over grey rocks; water, deep and green, in pools under the trees. He lapped at it, and woke and tried to lick cracked lips, but he had no saliva.

Water!

He needed it to save his life. He had not drunk for three days. He had tried to drink from the sheep trough, but the farmer, defending his water with his gun, had shot across the beast's back. The shot had grazed him, and the wound was sore.

Stiff-legged, the fox loped into town, sniffing the air. There was no water on the moors. There might be water in the gutters, in the endless streets. Sometimes he raided dustbins there.

He tried to swallow, but his throat was too dry.

The storm was mounting. Thunder rumbled continuously, lightning sheeted and forked and cracked. Terrified children screamed; dogs crept under beds, or into cupboards, anywhere out of the repeated glare, wanting only to hide their eyes in the dark.

The houses were awake. Red-eyed men in need of a shave went downstairs to make tea with the carefully husbanded water left from the day before. There would be no water until eight in the morning.

Water.

It was more precious than gold. More precious now than anything else that men possessed. It was worth stealing; worth fighting for. All suffered alike. Money could not buy an extra drink; money could not buy an extra bucketful; money could not fill the empty reservoirs.

In the valleys the once drowned houses stood up against the sky, ghost homes risen from the water; doors gaped empty, window frames held no glass; the tower of the old Norman church stood square again, and gulls roosted on the slimed green stones.

The rocks in the stream beds that fed the reservoirs were baked by the sun, and barely cool to the touch at night.

The fox crossed the dry stream bed. The rocks rolled beneath him. He slipped and fell, and lay still, exhausted, until lightning cleaved the dark again, and he dragged himself erect.

The way had never seemed so long. The path was endless. Step by slow step he crept along it, his body aching, his legs feeble, his heart pounding.

Suddenly, thin on the air, clear and cool, came the sound of a hunting horn.

The fox paused, one leg raised, ears pricked.

Clear and high, mellow and sweet.

The View Halloo.

And then the sound of a galloping horse and a long howling.

The fox ran.

He ran from memory. He ran from fear. He ran from terror. He ran from the baying of the hounds. He leaped the brook, though it had long forgotten water. He dived through bramble cover, tearing his fur and skin, so that his shoulder bled, and his dusty mask bled and there was a bead of blood on the end of his dry nose. He licked at it. It was wet.

He ran through a drainpipe and out at the other end.

He leaped along the trunk of a fallen tree and at the end of it cleared seven feet as he jumped to break his scent. He circled, but there was no water to foil the trail.

The horn sounded again.

In the church, the farmer's wife stared at the vicar and crossed herself. There had been no huntsman in the village for many years, though the children said that on stormy nights, when the lightning dazzled in a summer sky, he hunted again over paths he once had known so well.

The minister watched the lightning play on the walls, and listened to the thunder of phantom hooves and the sound of a phantom horn. He prayed for rain.

Father have mercy.

Thy children are sinful, but they know not what they do.

Gracious Lord, have pity on us.

Holy Father, send us rain; rain to drown the pestilence; rain to flood the reservoirs; rain to wash us clean again.

He thought of the days of his youth, spent with his father and mother in a far away mission house.

Swimming in a still lagoon; in a tropical sea, palm trees dark against a vivid sky. Then college in England, and a forest stream in a southern county, where the trout grew fat and flashed to the hook, silver arches with gleaming scales. Would there ever be fish again?

He thought of trees. Of deep green shade, and water dripping from the branches; of water streaming down the trunks, of raindrops dancing on the roof of the church.

There was a dry patter.

Was it rain?

He ran to the door to look out, forgetting the cat, who leaped up, startled and indignant, and then curled itself again at the base of the altar, not wishing to brave the noisy night.

It was not rain.

It was the dusty footsteps of a driven fox, fleeing from

a phantom horn. The beast ran down the road, and behind it came the soft shimmer of light, light that was hidden when the lightning flashed.

The horn sounded again.

Long, and low, and sad, calling to unseen hounds.

Hoofbeats thundered on the ground and behind them came the drumroll of thunder in the hills. Lightning flashed on an empty road, and a small fox, running, his strength almost spent.

The fox ran into the church.

The vicar closed the door.

The beast lay quiet, his sides heaving. His eyes closed. His dusty coat spread over the worn carpet, as if he had been spilled by a careless hand. His open mouth panted, sucking the dry air deep inside him.

There was a silver chalice on the altar.

Inside the cupboard were the precious bottles of holy water. The vicar took one, and opened it, and filled the chalice. The fox heard the sound, and opened his eyes, but he could not move. Exhaustion had claimed him.

The vicar could not allow the fox to die, there in his church, within reach of life.

Thunder rolled again.

The horn sounded again, faint and far away.

The old man sat on the edge of the pew, his knees aching from too long contact with the hard stone floor. The cat turned his head and saw the fox. He did not move. He had known thirst too.

The old man bent and set the chalice in front of the fox.

The farmer's wife watched, fascinated, knowing the fox was the enemy that raided her hen run; that took the dying lambs; that stole the water from the troughs. But she could not deny him drink.

Once again there was the sound of slow lapping.

The chalice was empty.

The old man filled it three times before the fox was done with drinking.

He ceased lapping.

But there was still a sound.

The sound of falling water. Of raindrops, hitting the

hard stone roof; beating on the pavements, slipping down the glass of the windows.

Rain!

The vicar flung wide the door. The fox ran into the night, and stood, rain beating against his coat, mouth lifted to the sky, rain falling into his throat, rain soothing his aching eyes.

Rain!

The cat ran into the rain and stood, mouth lifted too.

The vicar stood in the rain and the woman ran into the rain, feeling it wet against dry parched skin, wet against dusty hair, wet against clothes that had needed a wash for days.

People flocked into the rain, raced through the rain, held out their arms and lifted their faces, and then, driven by one thought, turned towards the church, wet and weary, a sodden army, to thank their God for the end of the drought.

The fox and the cat vanished into the night.

The farmer's wife crossed herself, and thanked her God, and walked through the night to the farm where she found her husband standing in the yard, his face turned up to the sky, a smile on his lips. He took her hand and they walked to the gate, and watched the cattle lift their heads too, and saw them move, and saw the old horse come out from beneath the trees, and stand rock still savouring rain.

Rain, to swell the streams and fill the reservoirs. Rain, to wash the cattle clean and lay the dust, and freshen the sere leaves of trees that had forgotten water.

Out on the moors, the fox stood in the growing stream, feeling the water cool dry pads and soothe aching bones. The cat lapped at a pool, knowing joy.

Even the rats drank.

The thunder died away. The lightning ceased to flash. Only the rain poured down, steadily, relentlessly, blessing the parched land.

In the church, the vicar spoke to a massed congregation.

The Lord moves in mysterious ways, his wonders to perform.

Voices lifted. Praise my soul, the King of Heaven.

The woman and the man in the farmyard heard it and echoed the words.

Only one child in the congregation did not sing. He was staring at a silver chalice that glittered on the worn carpet, and wondering why it was there.

The vicar saw it, and remembered, and smiled to himself.

He listened to the rain, and the far away sweet echoes of a hunting horn, and the beat of phantom hooves on the ground, and hoped that the fox was safe in his earth, and then he lifted his head and led the praise again.

He blessed the congregation.

They stood in the streets, faces lifted to the sky, unable to believe that now the drought was ended.

They brought out pans, and held them to fill.

Dawn brought a rainwashed sky, and the sound of birds, singing their own praises for water, a rising crescendo of ecstatic noise that continued long after the shadows had been chased away by light.

THE RAIDERS

The boy had been alone for much more than three hours.

He sat silent, in the dark house, listening. There was gunfire, far away. There were footsteps, and muffled sounds. And beside him was Marcus, his father's Alsatian, nine years old, and very wise.

The dog was listening too. He knew something that the boy did not yet know. The thread that bound him to his master, no matter where that master might be, had snapped suddenly and shockingly, a few hours ago.

He and the boy were now alone. Forever.

He knew where his master's body lay, and he wanted to go to it. The sound of shots had brought into being instincts that had been dormant for years, for the dog and the man had been a team, in wartime, slipping between the enemy lines, nosing out unseen trails, always avoiding man.

The dog raised his head and scented, his nose working, his brain analysing the smells he recognized, yet could never name. The men were drunk, and he knew from experience that the smell of drink meant harm for him; a kick, or a brick thrown hard, so that he had to run or he had to kill.

And he was not allowed to kill. The war was ended and he had been retrained.

He was a gentle dog, guarding a child; a wise dog, watching for danger; herding the little one, to see that he did not run into the road, or fall into the pool, or hurt himself in some other way.

Now he would have to kill if need be; to save the boy.

The boy had heard the shots, three hours ago. He had thought he heard the sound of the returning car; and then there was noise; angry shouts; and the quick bang-bang. And the dog had howled, under his breath, as if knowing he must not draw attention to them.

There were men all round him.

"One day, we may not come back," his father had said. "If that happens, get away. Trust Marcus. He will know what to do."

The big dog was waiting. Waiting for the men to go. But the men did not intend to go. They knew the boy was alone and they were trying to break his nerve.

It would be more fun, then.

They smoked and the lights were pin-points in the dark. Animal eyes, red and evil, waiting to kill.

The dog nosed the boy's leg.

The boy brought the lead, and together they crept out of the room, low on the ground, moving like shadows. There was the secret door that his father had made. If there were no men there, he could slip through, unseen, unheard.

Fear was souring his throat. His hands were slippery with sweat. The dog nosed him again and he drew back the bolt of the tiny trap that looked like a cupboard perhaps for garden tools, perhaps for an electricity meter, but nothing like an escape hatch from the house.

Night was too bright, the stars mocking him, the moon showing the path. Beyond the path was the forest. On the other side of the houses were the voices, careless now. He was only a boy, alone in an empty house, and they knew he was not yet thirteen years old. They did not know about the dog.

The dog could smell them; the smell was a reminder of many enemies; of night patrols, dodging the angry guns; of hours spent lying silent, hidden, while men tramped past. Men with bright eyes and fanatical faces and with death in their hands.

He led the way down the little path. The boy crept after him. He was wearing dark clothes, as he had been told. His father did not expect to live long. War was all around them. And worse, they no longer knew their enemies.

Beyond the path was the jungle, where snakes and tigers lurked, but he preferred to face the tigers. He could understand them. And the dog could kill the snakes. That too he had learned to do, running in swiftly to catch the beast behind the head and break the neck, while the poison fangs struck uselessly at the empty air.

Beyond the path his parents lay, side by side. The dog nosed his master. The boy looked down and the fear that lay heavily on him cramped his legs, and bile rose in his throat, but there were no tears. He was beyond tears.

He bent to look for his father's watch, to remember his father, but the watch was gone.

He dared not look at his mother.

The dog knew there was nothing left for him. He nosed the boy again and they slipped into the thickness of the trees, following the shadows. Even here there were men. The dog smelled the guns, and smelled the drink, and smelled the rank heady excitement that filled them with glee. They had forgotten civilisation and were once more warriors, ready to kill. Time had slipped away, leaving only the outer look of modern man.

The boy swallowed and pressed himself against the dog.

The dog led the way, moving carefully, avoiding open spaces. The boy's hands were stung by insects; his face was scratched by thorns; he was hungry and he was thirsty, but he dared not stop.

He did not know where the dog was leading him. He floundered through marsh; he bruised himself against hidden obstacles; he saw, through a gap in the trees, the flames that blazed from his deserted home, as the men, tiring of waiting, stormed it, and finding it empty, set it on fire. The smoke poured toward them, tarnishing the air.

Once a band of men came swiftly, running on tiptoe, and the Alsatian pushed against the boy, leading him to a little pool, where they crouched among the reeds, their scent destroyed by the water.

When the men went by, the boy heard the telltale pitpat of a dog's paws. Marcus had scented the dog and taken precautions against being discovered.

Night gave way to a grey dawn, to birdsong, and to brightness, and the dog led the boy to a dense thicket, well away from the main path. They slept there, the boy deeply, the sound sleep of exhaustion and terror, while the dog listened, ears moving, eyes watching, dozing, uneasy, only to wake and question the air again.

The wind changed.

Night came, and the dog knew that they were almost safe and that men had gone. But the boy was so tired he could only creep. His feet were bleeding and the stings on his body were burning him. So was his head burning him; fire raged in his cheeks, and he ached in every bone.

He stumbled and the dog nipped him, trying to bring him onto his feet again.

He could not.

He was lying there still when dawn came.

The dog raised his head and sniffed the air.

There was no danger now. The men had gone.

He raced along the path, emerging into the little clearing during the early-morning service, disrupting the prayers as he barked at the missionary. The man looked at the dog, and saw how the animal turned towards the forest again.

The men from the mission ran.

The boy was lying where the dog had left him. The men bent over him and lifted him, helping him to his feet.

"You are safe now," the missionary said.

The boy looked up at him, and reached out his hand to the dog, stroking his dense fur. The long tail waved happily. The Alsatian had done his duty.

He was safe among friends and would have food and shelter.

But the boy knew he would never feel safe again.

UNFORGOTTEN

In our memories they lie
Long after they die,
Those four-footed ghosts
To which, briefly, we're hosts.
They were all treasures,
The source of our pleasures
With gay waving tails
And glowing brown eyes.
They are our past,
These memories that last.
The dog in the ring,
Now he was a king,
And that sweet-natured bitch
Made us feel rich.
Time passes and heals,
But memory steals
And the dog at our side
Which we cherish with pride,
Noses our knee,
Saying "What about me?"
Aware for that moment,
We'd paused and we'd sighed,
As he triggered the memory
Of the great dogs that died.

THE LAKE

The willows
Stoop to the shining water.
A moorhen glides
Among trembling reeds.
The wild drakes chase one another,
Punishing the pool,
Quacking shrill challenge,
Vying for the timid ducks
Hiding under the bank.
A blackbird calls,
A sudden fluting.
Two magpies fly,
Rain speckles the lake.
Wind rustles the willows.
The wild duck shelter.
Nothing moves.
The only sound
Is the sigh of the wind in the trees
And the pit pat pit on the water.

THE HAWK

The hawk
Hangs on the air,
Amber eyes
Searching the heather.
A white scut flashes.
The bird plunges,
Talons outstretched,
Grey fur raking.
A sudden braking.
The hare jinks sideways,
The bird crashes

To the ground,
Feathers shuddering.
Recovering,
He soars.
Beneath him
Nothing moves.
The hare is hidden.
The bird flies to his nest,
Brooding,
Hungry.

THE FOX

White feathers
Drift over the grass,
Mute witness
Of night-time violence.
The red fox slinking,
A duck in his mouth.
Here he stayed, to feed
By the ruffled pool.
The willows shake in the wind.
The white ducks quake
In the rustling reeds.
Tonight they are safe.
What of tomorrow?

THE PEREGRINE FALCON

Bird soaring,
Hunger driving.
The sun shines
From a clear sky.

Wind shivers the branches.
A stir of movement.
The bird dives,
Cleaving the air.
His shadow grows,
Giant bird,
Darkening the heather,
Clouding the summer day.
A cry.
A quick kill.
The bird flies
To the dead tree
That spikes from the moor.
He drowses,
Full fed.
The canny hare
Creeps out of cover
And leaps across the ground,
Safe, for this moment.

THE GEESE

The grey geese
Nest in the swaying reeds.
The hunting vixen
Pounces.
There is a cackling on the water.
Grey bodies thrash the surface.
Wild waves ruffle the pool.
The hunter steals away.
The geese huddle,
Silent.
One lonely feather
Blows on the wind.
The silken shallows are still,
Untroubled by memory.